I0601837

Nora Perry

The Tragedy of the Unexpected

And other Stories

Nora Perry

The Tragedy of the Unexpected
And other Stories

ISBN/EAN: 9783744750165

Printed in Europe, USA, Canada, Australia, Japan

Cover: Foto ©Andreas Hilbeck / pixelio.de

More available books at **www.hansebooks.com**

THE

Tragedy of the Unexpected,

AND OTHER STORIES.

BY

NORA PERRY.

BOSTON:
HOUGHTON, MIFFLIN AND COMPANY.
The Riverside Press, Cambridge.
1880.

CONTENTS.

THE

TRAGEDY OF THE UNEXPECTED.

———◆———

"JIM, old man, what 's up?"

"I don't know 's anything is up," was the rather surly response to this question.

"Oh yes, there is, there 's been something to pay with you for the last three days, and you might as well out with it, for I tell you what, I can't stand this sort of thing any longer if you and I are to be joint occupants of this parlor."

"What sort of thing, I should like to know?" was the still more surly response to this appeal, accompanied by a sudden movement of the square shoulders and an upward fling of the bent head which brought into the light a face with a look of haughty questioning upon it. The other only laughed a little as he met this look; he did n't seem at all impressed by it; laughed, and presently went on : —

"No, I can't stand it, Jim. That 's a fact. You 've

done nothing but sit with your boot-heels jammed into that grate, and your eyes fixed upon both of those interesting objects to the exclusion of everything else, for the last three days.   And I 'm blessed if in that time you 've given me a civil answer. And now I want to know what 's up."

" I 'm very sorry if I 've disturbed you, Hamlyn, but I think a man might be allowed the liberty of being silent when he 's not in the mood for conversation, without being brought to book in this way."

Ned Hamlyn came round and laid his arm across the back of the chair in which his companion sat.

" Jim, you 're a trump of a good fellow at heart, but you 've got a beastly temper though, have n't you ? "

The good-natured insinuating affectionateness of this was indescribable.   It had a peculiar effect upon Jim Marlowe, for he suddenly dropped his head against the chair back, and lifting his eyes to the face above him, exclaimed with abrupt vehemence, —

" Good Heavens ! how like you are to her, sometimes."

" Yes, I know, you 've told me so before, Jim. And so the trouble 's there, is it — with Miss Alice ? I thought so."

" Yes, Alice and I have parted, Ned.   That 's what 's up."

"Quarreled, eh? Well, what's that! make it up again," advised the other, cheerfully.

"Easier said than done, when a woman tells you that she never wants to see you again."

"Whew! Well, that is rather strong, but see here, Marlowe, what had *you* been saying to *her?*"

Marlowe got up and stamped about the room. "Oh, I don't know, I don't know, Hamlyn. I don't suppose I was very amiable."

"I don't suppose so, either," remarked Hamlyn, half laughing.

"It all began about that little Colt — Tom Colt. We were up at my Aunt Ann's, Alice and I, and the Colts were there, the whole lot of 'em, — beggarly set. Colt — Tom — wanted to marry Alice, you know, and he's forever hanging round her whenever he gets a chance; and Alice, I think, takes a very mistaken way with him. She says she's sorry for him, and, well, really, she's so confoundedly pleasant to the little cub that he's got to be altogether too presumptuous, in my opinion. When I spoke about this to her the other night she disagreed with me, of course; and when we came to argue the matter she would n't listen to reason, — in fact, it was no argument whatever, and before I was in the least prepared for it I got my *congé.* That's the whole of the matter."

"Jim, somehow or other you've blundered awfully, for Miss Alice was very fond of you."

"I suppose a man always blunders when he disagrees with a woman," was the rather satiric reply.

"He blunders in the way he *expresses* his disagreement, generally; that's where the trouble is."

"I dare say. I dare say I made a fool of myself, and was unnecessarily abrupt."

"Well, this looks promising. Jim, try and recall one or two of these abrupt remarks of yours. I want to get at the bottom of this thing, and set you right."

"I don't know that I can recall the exact language I used, but I believe I conveyed to her that I thought her love of power and her vanity would seriously undermine her character if she was not careful, and not only destroy her own happiness but that of others."

Ned Hamlyn gave a long, low whistle, more eloquent than any words. Marlowe colored a little as he heard it. "Well, I suppose that means that you think I've been an arrogant prig, Hamlyn."

"Rather, — yes." A moment's pause; then, "Jim, I never saw such a fellow as you are to sit in judgment and pronounce on people. You may be in the right about it here, but to fling such a judgment straight in a woman's face! I don't much wonder, I confess, that Miss Raymond ordered you off."

" Ned, what do you mean by saying I may be right in my judgment here?"

" Only, that I don't know Miss Raymond well enough to dispute you."

" Alice Raymond is a very noble girl, Hamlyn."

" I always supposed so, and you talked to this 'noble girl' as if she were a school-girl, who needed your superior wisdom to reform her wandering steps, and set her in the right path."

" Hang it, Ned, don't make me out quite such a prig. I was hurt and sore, and I hated to see her demean herself by being friendly with that little whipper-snapper."

" Jim, you're a great deal cleverer than I am, lots of intellect and 'ability' and all that, but I know one thing, I should never have presumed to be so 'cock sure,' as that fellow in 'Friends in Council' says, that my judgment was so infallible when I was in a special state of irritation. I think I should have had a dim suspicion that my own shortcomings might weigh perhaps in the balance, and find me wanting in the power to measure another person."

" Of course you would, Ned. Intellect! Ability! Don't talk to me in that style; you're a long ways ahead of me, for it's *character* that tells, that makes the man. Ned, I've been an arrogant brute; you've made me see that very clearly. But I gen-

erally see things that are for my advantage too
late."

"Oh, you've given it all up then, and don't intend to ask Miss Raymond to forgive you?"

"I? Why she told me she never wanted to see
me again!"

Ned Hamlyn laughed in his pleasant, quiet way.
Then he remarked as quietly, —

"Jim, you don't know all you might, spite of
your cleverness. Perhaps when Miss Raymond
said that, she might have *thought* she meant it for
the moment; the next moment, when you were
out of her sight, it was a very different matter.
Women, nor men either, don't give up their loves
so quickly."

Marlowe, who had resumed his seat by the fire,
now turned squarely about, facing the light and
his friend.

"What are you driving at, Ned? What would
you have me do?"

"Write to her, and tell her that you see the
error of your ways. Confess yourself the brute
you have been in your conceit, and ask her to take
you back on trial."

Marlowe, for the first time during the conversation, smiled at this glib advice, so jauntily spoken.
But he knew that Hamlyn was thoroughly in earnest, and he knew that it was sound advice he had
given.

"Suppose she was more in earnest than you think, Ned, suppose she scorns me anew," was his suggestion to this advice.

"Well, I should think that worth the risking," was Hamlyn's reply, in a dry tone. In the little silence that followed, Hamlyn's sweet, clear tenor hummed softly, —

> "He either fears his fate too much,
> Or his desert 's too small,
> Who dare not put it to the touch
> And win or lose it all."

"Ned, you think I 'm rather a poor sort of fellow, don't you?"

"No, not usually, but," with a sudden accession of vehemence, — "I hate to see a man hang back, and afraid to risk anything where a woman 's concerned. It seems ungenerous at the best; and at the worst it 's a sneaking kind of caution that a manly man ought to be ashamed of."

"You 're quite right, Hamlyn, and I was n't thinking of caution in that way; I only felt that I could n't stand another blow from that quarter very well — and I could n't but hesitate at the prospect of going over the suffering of the last few days again."

"Yes, I see — and I beg your pardon, old fellow. All the same I don't think you need fear."

There was another space of silence, and then suddenly James Marlowe started from his chair and going forward to the writing table began to push away the newspapers that covered it with an alert movement of interest that spoke volumes. Hamlyn jumped up at this indication with a bright look of commendation. "That's it, Jim. Write to her at once; you'll never regret it. In the mean time I'll go out and keep an engagement I made with Peters. You don't need my advice or my company now."

When Jim Marlowe once made up his mind to do anything there was no shilly-shallying about it. He had made up his mind to write to Alice Raymond, and there was neither doubt nor hesitation as to what he should say from the beginning to the end of his letter. And this was the letter:—

DEAR ALICE,—I know now that I was very pig-headed and disagreeable in my way of putting things the other night, but will you try and forgive me, and say that I may come back again to you to prove my repentance and affection? I shall await your reply with great impatience, and am

Yours always,

JIM MARLOWE.

When Ned Hamlyn came in four hours' later, which was close upon midnight, he found his friend sitting in the very position about which he had chaffed him so unmercifully in the earlier part of the evening — with his boot-heels jammed into the grate. "Hullo, Jim, been sitting there in that cheerful manner ever since I left?"

"Ned, I sent my note to Alice ten minutes after you went out — sent it by Robert. I questioned him when he came back, and he said that he handed the note to the 'General' — old Dick, you know, the black fellow who's been in the family so long, and he promised that he would take it up to Miss Alice at once."

"Well, what then? Did you expect that she'd answer it to-night?"

"Yes, I did, Ned."

Ned Hamlyn gave one of his amused good-natured little laughs.

"For a man who was so utterly despairing and hopeless in one hour, to be so confident in the next" — another laugh finished the sentence.

"I suppose it does look over-confident, Ned, but my disappointment arose not so much from confidence in myself as in the fact that it was always Alice's way to respond immediately. The 'General' has brought me many a note in an hour after the receipt of mine."

"Yes, very likely; but, my reasonable young friend, I don't suppose the correspondence was exactly on such a basis as this, eh?" asked Hamlyn, with a quizzical look.

" Well, no, not exactly," jerked out Marlowe, with a short, unmirthful laugh.

" I thought so, my boy; consequently I should be content to wait, I think — certainly until daylight.   Perhaps by that time Miss Raymond's affection may get the mastery of her to such an extent that she will rout the ' General ' out of bed and send him off post-haste with full forgiveness, and an urgent invitation to your lordship to settle all your differences over a cup of coffee."

Marlowe smiled grimly at this burlesque, but it did him good, as Hamlyn's easy good-nature always did.

" Yes, I suppose I 'm an impatient fool," he said, "and that I need n't expect a reply until to-morrow."

" And in the mean time I should advise you to take your boot-heels out of that grate, and seek ' tired nature's sweet restorer,' as I intend doing without further delay; so good night, old man, and pleasant dreams of to-morrow's felicity."

II.

Bᴜᴛ there was no "to-morrow's felicity" in store for Jim Marlowe. The day came and went, and no reply to his frank and tender appeal appeared. When another and still another day dragged by with the same result, even Ned Hamlyn's happy optimism faltered a little. As for Marlowe himself, he went about.with a savage look of excited misery, that cut Hamlyn to the heart, and gave him no little anxiety into the bargain.

"He's just the fellow to do something rash or desperate in his present condition," he meditated, as he observed his friend's gloomy abstraction.

When a week had transpired, therefore, and Marlowe suddenly announced that he was going down to his uncle's place at Highwood for a month's visit, Hamlyn felt decided relief.

"It's the most sensible thing that you could do, Jim. Just the thing I should like to have suggested."

"I shall drive up to the city to my business every day with Uncle Tom, and return in the afternoon, so I shall see you now and then, Ned, though," with a faint smile, "my room will be a good deal better than my company for the present, I 'm thinking." There was a slight pause ; then, " If any letters come to our rooms for me you 'll send them at once to my office, — and — well — that 's all I believe. Good-by, old fellow."

Ned Hamlyn's good-by and hand-shake were like a jolly benediction. His thought, as Marlowe turned away, " Safe, now, by Jove ! " What he had feared he hardly knew himself, but, with a great affection for Marlowe, he had never been able to quite understand him, — they were too unlike for such understanding, — the unlikeness of opposites. which is the basis of friendships that never lose their charm. From this lack of understanding, therefore, often arose a feeling of perplexity in Hamlyn's mind in regard to Marlowe, when any crisis came up. He used to say laughingly, sometimes, " You are an unknown quantity to me ; I never know just how you are going to turn out." The right thing, however, had turned out now in this happy, easy-going optimist's opinion. " The most sensible thing that Jim could do," he thought, whenever his mind reverted to this visit. Perhaps for the first week after Marlowe's departure Hamlyn looked with some faint expectation for the letter that his friend had hinted at in that general direction of his about " letters." But this faint expectation did not last beyond that first week.   It was entirely out of his mind on the

second, and at the end of the third, when he came
whistling into their parlor one afternoon, and
found a square, cream-laid envelope upon the table,
inscribed, in the great waving chirography of the
present feminine fashion, to "Mr. James Marlowe;" he had for the time so absolutely put Miss
Raymond out of his mind that she did not recur to
him until he caught sight of the monogram upon the
seal. Then he stood quite still, glaring down upon
the graceful little cipher in a sort of dazed speculation for the space of half a minute or so. When,
presently, the truth and importance of the whole
matter penetrated his surprised consciousness he
dropped the letter upon the table with this emphatic ejaculation, "Thunder!" But he was not
a man to remain inactive long, however surprised,
and the next moment saw him dashing off down
town towards Marlowe's office with the important
missive in his pocket. But, as fate would have
it, Marlowe had been gone more than an hour.
" Went earlier to-day, sir," said the clerk ; " some
sort of a picnic going on at Highwood, I believe."

Hamlyn pulled out his watch. " Ten minutes to
five. If I can catch that five o'clock train it 's a
go," he said to himself. It was one minute past
five as he rushed into the Eastern depot, but the
train had been delayed and was just moving slowly
out of the building, giving Ned the opportunity

that the careless young American always finds sufficiently ample, to swing himself in break-neck
fashion upon the last car. When, half an hour
later, he jumped off at the little station at the foot
of the Highwood grounds, he hesitated a moment
in considering whether he had better take the direct way to the house, or strike across the little
meadow towards the woodland, where most likely
the picnic the clerk had spoken of, might then be
in operation. A murmur of voices decided him on
the latter course, for it came directly from over the
meadow-land. Following this track soon brought
him in view of the gay party just as they were
preparing to partake of their rather elaborate picnic banquet. So absorbed were they that Hamlyn
was close upon them before they were aware of his
proximity.

A charming girl in a pink-flowered gown and
a wide Devonshire hat, who looked to Hamlyn as
if she had stepped out of an old picture-frame, was
the first to spy him. She was standing in a half-
drooping attitude, putting apparently the finishing
touches to the decorations of the rustic table. A
gentleman, whose back was towards Hamlyn, was
evidently assisting her. But Hamlyn did not give
him more than a vague observation. His attention was wholly concentrated upon the girlish face
confronting him, and this not merely by reason of

its beauty, but for the singular intentness, the wistful inquiry, that seemed to look out of the soft eyes. In a moment, however, a new expression mingled with the wistfulness as she said something to her companion. "Lovers!" commented Hamlyn, concisely, as he watched the change in her face. At that instant the gentleman turned quickly.

It was Jim Marlowe.

"Why Ned, is it you? You're just in time. Glad to see you, old fellow." Marlowe was evidently a trifle surprised at Hamlyn's unexpected appearance, but glad to see him as he had said. With his hand still grasping Ned's he introduced him to the girl in the Devonshire hat. "My friend, Mr. Hamlyn, Miss Amherst." All the wistfulness had now quite gone out of Miss Amherst's face. She laughed joyously as she greeted Mr. Hamlyn. "I thought you were a telegraph messenger, Mr. Hamlyn," she cried lightly, "you looked so anxious."

"Well, I am not very tall, but I did n't think I was down to the average of a telegraph boy," responded Hamlyn, as lightly.

"Oh, but I assure you that our messenger at Highwood here, stands certainly five feet seven, and that is n't a very boyish stature, Mr. Hamlyn," quickly replied Miss Amherst.

"Oh, that's Lannerkin, Marlowe; Miss Amherst took me for Tom Lannerkin;" and Hamlyn laughed mischievously as he recalled the dandy Irishman who used to tell people solemnly that he was one of the telegraph company's officers. Miss Amherst was about to respond to this when some one called her. As she stepped forward, Hamlyn, with a motion of his head, drew Marlowe aside, and hastily said, "I've a letter for you, Jim; found it when I went home to our rooms this afternoon. You'd been gone an hour, Walker told me, when I got to the office, and I had just time to catch the five o'clock train."

Marlowe flushed, then turned pale, and the hand with which he took the letter shook as with an ague chill there in the June afternoon. The two walked on a few paces together, then, recollecting himself, Marlowe muttered a quick "Wait for me a moment, Ned," and returned to make his excuses to Miss Amherst for leaving her. Hamlyn could not hear what he said, but he saw his air of constraint, and heard Miss Amherst exclaim, —

"Oh, it *is* bad news then!" There were a few more words, and then Marlowe rejoined him. A short walk brought them into a shaded retreat, out of sight and sound of the picnickers, and Hamlyn turned away as his friend broke the seal of his letter. The moment of silence was broken, presently,

by a smothered ejaculation, — a moment more, and
Marlowe cried out, " Ned, look here."   The voice
was broken, and there were tears in Jim Marlowe's
eyes.

" What, she has n't waited all this time to turn
upon you ? " blurted out Hamlyn, taking fire at his
companion's unwonted exhibition of emotion.

" Turned upon me!   Ned, she 's been ill, — was
ill when my note reached the house, — down with
typhoid fever, and knew nothing of it, in fact, until
yesterday.   She has only written a word or two,
and her sister adds another word, — begs me to
come to Alice at once."

" You 'll go back on the train with me, then, —
starts in just an hour, — at seven.   Don't look so
forlorn, old man; Miss Raymond is young, and
will pull through this."

Marlowe looked as if he had n't heard a word
that Hamlyn had said.

" I shall go up on the train with you at seven;
but you don't understand, Ned, what a blundering,
brutal fool I have been."

" Oh well, don't worry about that, Jim.   It 's all
over, and it 's all right now."

" Is it!   My God, Ned, what do you suppose I
have done to make everything all wrong ?   I offered
myself last night to Lucy Amherst ! "

2

" Thunder ! " ejaculated Ned Hamlyn, for the second time that afternoon.

" And I am going to town with you in an hour from now to see Alice Raymond ! " continued Marlowe, in a tone of almost fierce defiance, as " who shall dare to say I should n't ? "   " Can I do otherwise ? " he resumed presently.   " Look at it.   Alice has been very ill, is now very weak, and has set her heart upon my coming to her, poor darling," — his voice breaks a little here; " if I fail to go I may do worse mischief than I have yet achieved, don't you see ? "

" Yes, I suppose it 's the only thing to do now ; but what about Miss Amherst ? " asks Ned, rather dubiously : " shall you tell her, shall you explain anything, — where you are going, you know ? "

" No ; I must have more time.   Lucy is like a child in some things.   I could not enter into explanations now.   But, Ned, I want to tell you how all this happened.   When I came down here I did n't know that Lucy Amherst was to be here ; not to say that that fact would have made any difference.   But she is Uncle Tom's ward, and his great favorite.''

" Ah, I see.   This is the young lady he wanted you to marry ? "

" Exactly."

" I saw another thing, Jim, — that Lucy Amherst

was very much in love with you. But you are not
in love with her, — you never have been; not even
last night, when you offered your valuable self to
her. Now would you mind telling me what possessed you to do so?"

"Ned, I have been trying to get away from all
my recollections for these three past weeks; to
get away from myself and my misery; to drown
thought, and take up a new life. I met Lucy Amherst here, saw her day after day, and — well, last
night I saw that perhaps I might make another
happy, and finally find relief and contentment myself, in that."

"Lord! Jim, when you went off three weeks
ago I said to myself it was the most sensible thing
you could do. I thought you were safe then, for
I'd had a fear all along that you were capable of
any rashness. Safe! And here you've been getting into this fix."

"You can't be harder on me than I am on myself, Ned. But remember, I had given up all hopes
in the other direction. I thought all was lost there,
and — I was desperate."

"I don't mean to be hard on you, old man, that
is n't what I meant; it's only that I'm so awfully
sorry for you."

"You 're the best fellow in the world, Ned; the
best friend a man ever had. If I could take on

something of your temperance and serenity of nature I should be a wiser as well as a happier man."
As he spoke Marlowe laid his hand affectionately
on the other's shoulder, and the two sat thus together, saying little, until they were suddenly surprised by a sound of voices, and in another moment
Miss Amherst and a young companion stood before
them.

"Mr. Hamlyn, what do you mean by running
away with your friend in this manner, or what does
your friend mean by running away with you?"

Her tones were laughing, but there was an anxious look in her face.

Marlowe went forward a step or two to meet
her. "Lucy, Hamlyn has brought me some news
which may turn out very bad news if I don't go to
town at once — to see about it. Will you excuse
me to all the rest, and say to Uncle Tom that I
sha'n't be back to-night! Come, walk up to the
house with me, — we must be off at seven. Hamlyn," looking over his shoulder to that young
man, who was considerately occupying the attention
of Miss Amherst's companion, "perhaps, if Miss
Wilder will show you the path, you might as well
be on your way to the station now, by the brook
bridge; we have n't much time, and you have had
enough of hurrying for one night, with the thermometer at seventy-eight."

Hamlyn turned away with Miss Wilder, — that sprightly young woman glancing mischievously at her escort to see if he appreciated " the situation," as she termed it. All the way to the station she was full of her airy little gayeties. At another time Ned Hamlyn would have found her " a nice, jolly little thing," but now she jarred upon him, and he thought impatiently, " Lord, what fools girls are ! "

III.

A week after this, Ned Hamlyn received through the post a very dainty-looking little missive inscribed in a delicate feminine hand. He was in something of a hurry, and tossed it down at the first glance with the words, " Another of those confounded Kettledrums, I suppose, where a fellow loses his dinner for a lot of flum." A second thought made him pick it up again ; opening it, this is what he read : —

" Will Mr. Hamlyn be so kind as to call upon Miss Amherst between the hours of six and seven on Wednesday afternoon."

This brief note was dated from Miss Amherst's city home, and postmarked that very morning — Tuesday, the 20th. Hamlyn had, therefore, plenty of time to ponder all the contingencies and possibilities. It had clearly something to do with Marlowe and his absence from Highwood. Why the dickens, then, had n't she sent for Jim? This was one of the annoyed queries that Hamlyn put to himself during the interval that transpired before the time of the appointed interview. When, on Wednesday, he stood in the long, dim parlor awaiting Miss Amherst's coming, he had perhaps never felt so thoroughly uncomfortable in his life. He had a vague idea that there was to be a painful scene of some description, in which he must enact the double part of tale-bearer and comforter. "Lord! I wish it was over," he thought nervously, as he fidgeted about the room. Just then he heard the soft rustle of a woman's garments, and the next instant Miss Amherst stood before him.

"I am very sorry to have kept you waiting, even for a moment, Mr. Hamlyn," began the young lady so quietly and composedly that Ned felt his nerves steady a little: "what I wanted to say to you was about Mr. Marlowe. I know that you are his most intimate friend and that you are aware of — our — of what he had said to me the night before he left us." She paused an instant, and Hamlyn nodded a grave assent. "When he left me that night he said no more to me of the cause of his absence than you heard. He has written to me almost daily since, however, saying that he would see me very soon and explain more fully. I should have waited patiently, and spoken to no one of my anxiety, if something I heard yesterday did not suggest to me that I ought at once to know the truth that I might act upon it. I knew, of course, that Ja — Mr. Marlowe had been engaged to Miss Raymond; that it was broken off with no possibility of renewal. Yesterday, however, my cousin came to me and told me that Miss Raymond had been very ill; that Mr. Marlowe had been sent for by her request; and that he was now in daily attendance upon her. Mr. Hamlyn, will you tell me whether this is true? I think I ought to know."

" Yes, I must admit that it is true, Miss Amherst; but you must remember that Miss Raymond knew nothing of Mr. Marlowe's recent engagement to you."

"I know. I am blaming nobody. But she had broken off — had refused all communication with Mr. Marlowe. He was quite free, everything was at an end between them when — he spoke to me."

"He supposed so," answered Hamlyn, uneasily.

"Ah! Mr. Hamlyn, tell me all the facts. I ask you this not because I have no confidence in Mr. Marlowe, but" — a deep blush rising and overspreading her face — "because I have no confidence in myself in a certain matter."

With a good many hesitations Hamlyn related what he knew. It was impossible, of course, to do this without revealing more or less of Marlowe's suffering.

Miss Amherst heard him quite to the end with no interruption of question or comment. She was silent a moment after he had ceased speaking, then, with a remnant of the fiery blush still on her cheek in two burning spots, but with the same controlled voice, she said, "You have done me a great service, Mr. Hamlyn, and I thank you." The next moment she had risen to her feet, and Hamlyn knew that the interview was over, even before she concluded in the same tone of courtesy, "I know that you will pardon me for the great liberty I have taken, and for detaining you so long on what must be a very disagreeable business to you."

When Hamlyn found himself on the street once more, it was with a feeling as if he had been playing a part in a very curious dream. He had expected a scene, and had fortified himself against it. He had expected to meet a high-strung, emotional girl, who would have no consideration whatever for the annoyance she might be inflicting upon a third party in the absorption of her own trouble. He had, instead of assisting at a scene, been the second in a very calm little business interview, the principal in which, instead of being an emotional, demonstrative young lady, was a self-possessed woman, who had made him of use to herself, and then dismissed him with the graciousness of a queen, without so much as revealing a glimpse of her own motives, or the action she meant to take upon the facts he had given to her. " Of course," meditated the young man as he considered all this, "the fire is smoldering underneath, and Marlowe has got to meet it. Well, I must say she has shown herself a remarkably well-bred young person, as far as I am concerned."

Hamlyn had not by any means an overweening curiosity in regard to other people's affairs, but it must be confessed that he felt considerable interest in the affair which had so oddly wound him up in its meshes, and was not a little desirous of seeing the upshot of it all. He would not question Marlowe, however, until his friend opened the matter again, neither would he be the first to mention his strange interview with Miss Amherst. He had seen very little of Marlowe, however, since his return. They were the joint occupants of the same parlor in the hotel where they made their home, but each had a separate bedchamber in quite another part of the house, so that it not unfrequently happened that several days went by without their being very much in each other's society. It did, however, seem a little queer to Hamlyn when three days had elapsed after his talk with Miss Amherst, without his hearing a word from Marlowe concerning it, for what did that young woman desire the facts she sought so earnestly, but to confront her quondam suitor with them, and come to some settlement thereby. Hamlyn was pondering over this point quite intently on the third evening, when Marlowe made his appearance, bearing an open letter in his hand, and wearing upon his face a mingled look of admiration and astonishment.

"Ned, read that," handing him the letter.

Hamlyn at once, at the first glance, recognized the flowing characters of Miss Amherst. He thought he could pretty accurately judge of the reproachful contents. But this is what he read :—

DEAR MR. MARLOWE, — I have just had an interview with Mr. Hamlyn, which I sought myself, that I might ask him if the rumor that my cousin brought to me at Highwood of Miss Raymond's illness and your constant attendance upon her, was true. I pressed Mr. Hamlyn to tell me the whole truth, because I felt that, whatever it might be, it was better for me to learn it through him than through you. He has told me enough for me to understand everything. I do not blame you, — you thought that you were free when you asked me to be your wife, and you were not. It would have been better if you had told me at once when you heard from Miss Raymond, but I can see that you meant kindly in not doing so, for you did not know that I could be trusted. I hope Miss Raymond is better, that she will soon be quite restored, and that you may be happy, for I see now that you could only be happy with her; that however kind or tender you might be to another, she alone has your heart. It is not best for us to meet again; but when I say this do not think I feel hardly towards you, — you have meant everything kindly where I was concerned, — circumstances only have been trying, and have put us both in positions which have brought about a mutual suffering which seems cruel now. But that will pass in time, and I shall never think of you but as your true friend   Lucy Amherst.

"By Jove!" was the only exclamation that for the moment expressed Hamlyn's astonishment and admiration. The next moment he added, "And this is the girl you thought was to be treated like a child. Jim, men don't know much about women, after all. This is a revelation that makes me feel as if we were poor creatures beside them."

"Very poor," responded Jim Marlowe, emphatically.

There was a little pause, broken at last by Hamlyn, who inquired, in rather a subdued voice, "Have you told Miss Raymond — about — about Miss Amherst?"

"No; Alice was too weak from her illness, it would n't have been safe. Ned, I somehow seem to have been playing a very weak, ignoble part all through. I ought, as Lucy Amherst says, to have told her everything long before, but on the day that I received Alice's note I was so startled, so shaken by the sudden news, and the whole matter was so confusing, so uncertain ; and when I had seen Alice, and found how imperatively I was needed to win her back to life, my days were so full, my mind in such a tumult, that I put off the explanation which was Lucy's right at once, because, I suppose, I was a miserable coward, who did not dare to shoulder any more responsibility."

"Well, I don't know," replied Hamlyn, thoughtfully; "they were, as Miss Amherst says, very trying circumstances, and I think any man might have waited and blundered a little."

"You 're a comforting fellow, Ned," returned Marlowe, smiling, but with a good deal of emotion in his voice. Hamlyn glanced across at the dark, moved face for an instant, but gave no other response to these words. He knew quite well the "tumult of thought" that was agitating his friend ;

but it was something they could not discuss together, gentlemen that they were, this great love of Lucy Amherst's, that had revealed itself so nobly and unselfishly in the simple lines she had written.

IV.

A YEAR from this time Hamlyn was Mr. and Mrs. Marlowe's guest at Highwood, where they were temporary host and hostess during the absence of Uncle Tom and his family in Europe. Marlowe had been married six months, and the happy occupant of Highwood about half of that period. Hamlyn, upon whom Lucy Amherst had made an ineffaceable impression, used to wonder now and then, as he roamed over the old place, how much or how little Marlowe recalled the days of the summer previous, when Lucy Amherst was his companion. But since that evening, a year ago, her name had not been mentioned between them. One day this admirer of Miss Amherst found himself wandering down through the little glade that led to the brook, with Mrs. Marlowe alone, for his companion.

" You have never been in this part of the place before, have you?" inquired Mrs. Marlowe, *en passant*, as they followed the narrow path.

"Yes, I think so; is n't this the way to the station?"

"Yes, but we have never taken this way. It 's only serviceable when one is in the woods."

"I know, but when I was here last summer, Miss Wilder, a pretty girl, who was visiting here, brought me through this short cut."

"Oh, I did n't know that you were staying here last summer."

"I was not. I came down on an errand one day, and it happened to be a day when they were all in the woods."

Suddenly, at these words, a sort of a flash of intelligence went over Alice Marlowe's face.

"Mr. Hamlyn, let me ask you, — was it the day you brought my note to Jim?"

"It was."

They walked on for a few moments after this in silence. Presently they stood upon the little bridge. A rustic seat had been built along on one side of it. "Let us sit here and rest for a while," said Mrs. Marlowe, and, suiting the action to the word, she gathered up her muslin skirts and deposited herself and them upon the little bench. She made a careless remark or two upon the beauty of the landscape, and then, with some quickness of speech and a heightened color, "Mr. Hamlyn, I have always wanted to speak to you about — about that time, and — Lucy Amherst."

Ned bowed acquiescingly, and his hostess resumed her subject by inquiring, —

" Did you admire Miss Amherst very much, Mr. Hamlyn ? "

" I had never seen her before that day of the picnic, and but once afterwards — yes, I admired her, of course," answered Ned, rather in the dark as to Mrs. Marlowe's meaning.

"Oh yes, I understand," was her quick response, in the tone of a person who thinks, " oh, if that is all, I can free my mind." And with a certain change both of tone and manner, a kind of expansiveness, she went on, " I knew that she came to you, and that you were aware of all the facts in the matter. James did not tell me directly ; I was too weak ; and even when he did, it was such a shock to me."

" Of course."

" Men are so different from women, Mr. Hamlyn. I could never have tried to replace him so quickly."

" Jim was very unhappy and very hopeless just then."

" And he consoled himself by allowing another woman to make love to him," returned Mrs. Marlowe with a laugh which had a ring of bitterness in it.

Hamlyn started, and stared at his hostess ; but

she did not observe him. "And the letter that she wrote after she discovered how matters stood was the most adroit piece of composition that I ever saw. No woman who loved a man with the depths of a deep nature could give him up so calmly; but it had its effect. James thought and still thinks that it is one of the noblest of letters, written from one of the noblest and most unselfish hearts in the world, and of course he suffered accordingly, for what he called his selfish impatience of his own misery, that made him rush into the affair so recklessly. But I don't think he *did* rush in. Lucy Amherst was always very much pleased with James, very fond of his society, and his Uncle Tom, you know, furthered everything of that sort. It was perfectly natural for him to do as he did, I am sure, under the circumstances. Don't suppose, Mr. Hamlyn, that I am, or ever was, jealous of Lucy Amherst: oh no. We are very happy, Jim and I, but I hate to have him think as he does, because it is always such a sore point with him, and he suffers from what he mistakenly supposed he made Lucy Amherst suffer, don't you see? And don't you agree with my view of the matter, Mr. Hamlyn?" She turned inquiringly to Hamlyn as she asked this question. A sound of footsteps in the grass arrested and diverted her attention. Hamlyn saw a bright, welcoming smile light up her face. "There he is now. Jim!" she called.

"Thank heaven!" breathed Hamlyn, devoutly, "I 'm out of that."

Going back to town a little later, he breathed a second thanksgiving that there would be no other opportunity to repeat the suddenly interrupted question. And leaning back in his seat he looked out upon the fields and meadow-lands of Highwood as the train sped past them, and thought involuntarily of the summer before, and Lucy Amherst in her Devonshire hat under those very trees glancing wistfully at Jim Marlowe, for whom she had smoothed out all the cruel difficulties of his own making, wherein she had been sacrificed, that he might peacefully marry another woman. And this other woman, this "noble girl" of whom everybody had seemed to think such fine things, had grudged Lucy Amherst even the grain of tender, grateful reverence which proved her husband's manliness. "By George, what an unexpected turn this 'view of the matter' from his Alice must have been to Jim!" concluded Hamlyn, as he got to this point of his meditations. "And, come to look at it, how unexpected everything has been through the whole affair. I declare," he suddenly soliloquized, as the train steamed into the station, "if I were a writer for the papers I would make a story of it all, and call it, THE TRAGEDY OF THE UNEXPECTED."

MRS. STANHOPE'S LAST LODGER.

RS. ARNOLD STANHOPE, or, as some persons persisted in calling her, Mrs. Stanup, eked out her narrow income by taking lodgers. Six years before, her husband had died and left her a fine old house at the West End, and just five thousand dollars besides. At the best percentage this was very little with which to take care of herself and her three children — children whose ages ranged from thirteen to seventeen, and whose education was then unfinished. At the first crisis Mrs. Stanhope took counsel with herself and her relatives.

"Sell the house and take a smaller one out of town, on a horse-car route, Kate," they one and all advised.

What was their amazement when, after listening to them in apparent heedfulness and respect, she coolly informed them that she had concluded to keep the house and rent her rooms to lodgers. "Kate, you are crazy!" exclaimed her brother-in-law. "This house and lot, in this locality, would bring you fifteen thousand any day. And with that sum well invested, and with what you have, you can live very nicely out of town."

" But I don't want to live out of town, Tom," she answered.

" We don't want to do a good many things that we are obliged to do in this world," Tom Alroyd retorted, a little impatiently.

" Well, I 'm not obliged to do this," Mrs. Stanhope returned, rather proudly. " It 's a matter of opinion, and I prefer to keep the house. As you say, it is in a very desirable locality. It will be no less desirable for lodgers."

" A matter of opinion, as you declare, Kate ; but I should hardly have thought that *you* would have *preferred* to fill your house with lodgers."

Then Mrs. Stanhope flashed out all there was in her mind.

" Tom, you may think me wild or Quixotic, or what you like. But, until I am actually obliged to, I will never give up the old Stanhope estate. My Harry is the last male descendant of the name. I know it was his father's desire that he should succeed to it, as he had done before him. And, besides that, I have a sentiment about it myself, I am proud of the old place, and I want to keep it in the family. Much too proud to let it go, Tom, though you may think I demean myself by taking lodgers."

This settled the matter. Tom Alroyd had nothing more to say, of course, but he nevertheless felt a good deal both of disapproval and annoyance. To his wife Mr. Alroyd prophesied all manner of ill-success to Mrs. Stanhope's plan. Kate was not a business woman. She would lose money. She would be taken in, in all sorts of ways, and lead a vexed and disturbed life, when she might lead such an easy one, comparatively, by following his advice. And the rest of the relatives, hearing this, thought Kate was " so foolish to run against Tom's advice — Tom, who was such a safe counselor in all business matters."

Long before the end of the six years when my story opens, Tom Alroyd was forced to confess that Kate had done better than he thought she would. She had certainly made both ends meet, and she had saved a little. If she was ever taken in, if she was ever vexed and disturbed by the way of life she had chosen, her relatives were none the wiser for it. She never complained to them. At the end of the six years Harry was nineteen, in his senior term at college, and with a good chance before him in a great commercial house, whose firm had known his father, and therefore felt an interest in the son. Harry was nineteen. Then came Ellen, who was two years older; and then Frances, or, as she was always called, Frank, with another two years of seniority.

When Ellen was twenty she considerably surprised her relatives by developing a talent for school-teaching. So, at least, she spoke of it, when she walked in one day with the information that she had been offered a situation in one of the grammar schools at a salary of $600. " I always suspected I had a talent for this thing, mother, and you see other people have suspected it too." She never told how she had been waiting for "this thing" for a year, and how this patient waiting and a really splendid scholarship, and, last but not least, the influence of an influential man, who had been Arnold Stanhope's intimate friend, had at the end of the year given her the situation she had sought. She was like her mother in this, that she never made a great thing of what she was doing; never talked about it, and laid before anxious friends her hopes and her fears and her patient womanly virtues. But her mother, who knew what silent courage and persistence she was possessed of, guessed that she had been working hard in many ways for " this thing," and at the last spoke of it in this *riant* manner to cover her real anxiety and perhaps distaste for it. And so she glanced up quickly at Ellen's information and asked her a plain question, while she watched her with searching eyes.

" Are you sure you have a talent for this, Ellen? do you like it? and shall you be happy in it? Because, if you do not, there is no necessity for it, remember that; for you are not as expensive nearly as you were as a school-girl, you know, and I managed then very nicely. Besides, you are valuable as a helping-hand in the care of the house."

Ellen colored a little at this, for she knew what her mother had thought. But she answered honestly enough, "I really think I have the talent, mother, and I dare say I shall like it; you'll let me try, won't you?"

"Oh yes, if you really are in earnest."

That was all the preliminary talk they had about it. And the next week the young teacher had entered upon her duties.

"What started you so suddenly on that track, Elly?" asked young Harry, rather grandly.

"Oh, my talent, Harry. I couldn't hide it in a napkin, you know, any longer." And Elly laughed.

"You see, Elly," Harry went on, still more grandly, "in another year I shall be able to take care of myself and do something for the rest of you, I dare say. So there is no need of your doing this thing."

"Thank you, Harry, you are very kind," answered Ellen, with a slight twinkle in her practical eye at Harry's swift surety of "doing something for the rest of you." "You are very kind, Harry, but there's my talent! I'm a little strong-minded,

you know, and I must work out what there is
in me."

Not until a year after this did any one know just
what it was that had started her on "that track."
But on the day that she was twenty-one, her uncle Tom was gayly bantering her as was his custom.

"If Harry stood in your shoes now, Miss Ellen,
it would be worth while. But I can't see why girls
should ever be twenty-one. They should keep in
their teens, you know, while they are girls. Why,
there's your mother and your aunt here were married off long before your age. Let's see, Kate;
you were only eighteen, and Mary was but seventeen. Why, what are you two about — you and
Frank? — nice-looking young women like you,
too."

Ellen answered this with great apparent careless-
ness; and you would never have thought, as she
answered, that she was at all disturbed. Frank,
who had been playing softly and fitfully at the
piano, heard this last remark of Uncle Tom's.
Pretty, vehement Frank, who looked much younger
than Ellen, but who was two years older, swung
herself round on the music-stool and cried out in
her little funny, quick-tempered way : —

"How can you talk in that style, Uncle Tom?
As if a woman's whole earthly concern was to get

married! I don't think you need be so proud of early marriages in our family if mother's and Aunt Mary's *did* turn out well. There's Aunt Harriet's: charming match that is, is n't it? And there's Uncle Dick, great splendid fellow tied to that little doll! Do you suppose if Aunt Harriet had waited until she was in her twenties she would have fallen in love with a man who murders the English language every time he opens his mouth? And do you think Uncle Dick would have married only a pretty doll if he had waited until he was a man?"

Uncle Tom Alroyd was n't very much pleased with this sudden attack; and there might have ensued quite a tilt of tongues if Harry had not just then come in with a "bee in his bonnet." When Harry had "a bee in his bonnet" it always buzzed very noisily without regard for time or place.

"I say, mother," he burst out, " Rob Barker's uncle is coming home from Europe, and Rob wants to get a room for him at the West End here. And I told him I guessed he could have Marchant's room. Marchant's going away, you know, next month."

" *Mr.* Marchant, Harry. Don't get into that flippant way of calling a man twice or three times your age ' Marchant.' It sounds under-bred," reproved Mrs. Stanhope.

"Well, Mr. Marchant, then. But about the room, mother?" persisted Harry.

"How old a man is Rob Barker's uncle, Harry?" asked Mrs. Stanhope, thoughtfully.

"Old? Well, he can't be very young; he stands in the place of Rob's father, you know."

"Oh!"

There was a satisfactory note in this "Oh!" which Mr. and Mrs. Alroyd understood perfectly; and the moment they were outside the door they commented upon it freely.

"There's another of Kate's queer quirks, Tom," said Mrs. Alroyd to her husband. "The idea of her setting her face against any lodger entering her house who is n't elderly!"

"She's afraid people will say she's after a husband for one of her daughters; Is n't that it?"

"Yes. She always remembered what Dick's silly little wife said to her at the outset."

"What was that?"

"Why, that she need n't trouble herself to dress Frank and Ellen for parties when they grew up; that they 'd find plenty of suitors in her lodgers. It was part malice and part earnest with Matty. You know she was always ashamed of Kate's taking lodgers."

"Pshaw! Kate's morbid!" exclaimed Mr. Alroyd.

"To be sure she is. I always said she was," Mrs. Alroyd returned.

And while they criticise Mrs. Stanhope's " queer quirks," as they styled her sensitiveness and pride, up stairs in their own room Frank and Ellen were having their little tilt of criticism.

" Oh ! " shivered out Frank, pulling down her long, shining hair with an impatient jerk, " I do get so very mad at Uncle Tom's speeches about marriage. I think it 's vulgar to talk in that way, Elly."

" Of course it is," answered the cooler " Elly," with more emphasis than usual. " Uncle Tom evidently thinks it 's a girl's bounden duty to marry *somebody;* or, at least, he thinks it 's *our* bounden duty. I fancied he 'd stop that kind of talk when he saw that I was able to take care of myself."

" Elly ! " — and Frank ceased her busy combing as the new thought struck her — " Elly, I do believe it was Uncle Tom's exasperating speeches that first set you thinking of taking care of yourself, as you call it."

Elly colored a little and laughed a little.

" Well, I suppose it was, Frank. It set me thinking in various ways. I saw that mother did n't need but one of us to assist her about the house. I felt that we were being 'talked at' a good deal in the matrimonial key, both by Uncle and Aunt Tom. It occurred to me that school-teaching would help the matter all round. But Uncle Tom does n't appear to believe much in that kind of help, I see. He seems to think that the only decent way for a woman is to get married," and Elly laughed again with the old gleam of humor in her eyes.

"Just to think of your earning $600 a year, Elly; you who are two years younger than I. You always were a great deal brighter than I, Elly. Bless my soul! I don't believe I am sound on my multiplication-table to this day. And when I go shopping I always have to count my fingers in my muff when I reckon up my change; I do, truly."

Elly laughed out at this, and Frank, meeting her amused look, laughed too.

" All I can do is to sweep and dust and make beds, and sometimes fuss round in the kitchen when Bridget is away. I have n't an acquisition or an accomplishment — not one. As far as that goes I 'm a fool." Then making an indescribable grimace at herself in the mirror, she concluded emphatically, " Yes, I 've got it — I 'm a healthy fool — just that."

Quiet Elly was laughing by this time as nobody but Frank could make her laugh. But as quick as she found her breath she said, animatedly, —

"How can you talk so, Frank, when you play so beautifully, and sing, too, like nobody else."

"'Like nobody else'— yes, that is the way, Elly, precisely; there's no training or science about it to make it like anybody else. And as for the playing, that's in the same category."

"I heard Mrs. Raymond say the other night that there was no playing or singing touched her like yours," answered Elly, quietly.

"*Did* she say that?" exclaimed Frank, her eyes all aglow — for Mrs. Raymond was great authority, a woman whose fine natural taste had been cultivated to the utmost. They talked awhile of this, and then dropped their voices as they heard the key in the room below them click in the lock. "I'm glad Mr. Marchant's going," said Frank in her lower tone; "he's such an old Betty. I've got tired of creeping round the house and talking in whispers for fear of disturbing him. Anyway, Elly, I think it's awful dull and poky to have a house filled with a parcel of old fusses. I *do* think mother is over-sensitive there. She says with two daughters like us it is better taste and better dignity to have quiet, elderly people in the house. I don't know but it is, but it's awful dull," reiterated Frank, shaking her head pathetically. "And no sooner does one go than another of the same sort comes. I should think they'd call it the Patriarchs' Retreat by this time," went on this droll little Frank, with a suppressed giggle.

"Hush! speak lower!"

"Oh, nobody can hear!" Then for a minute Frank was silent; but just as Ellen was falling asleep she heard her voice again: "Elly! Elly!" she whispered, "I wonder if Rob Barker's old uncle will come!"

"Stop talking, Frank, and go to sleep — do, dear — I'm so tired!" Elly remonstrated. And Frank went to sleep, and dreamed that Rob Barker's uncle was a greater fuss than all the rest; that he insisted on the house being still at nine o'clock; that he corked all the windows and listed all the doors; and that he capped the climax of this by entering a protest against her piano and Harry's flute. A month after this, when she had forgotten all about her dream, she came in one day to find the house in quite a commotion. Not only Mr. Marchant's vacant room was being metamorphosed, but the side-room opening out of it.

"Oh, Granny Barker's coming, I suppose, in place of Granny Marchant," she said to herself, as she caught sight of Rob Barker in the chaos of pictures and furniture. "And the old gentleman is to have two rooms!" she went on with her inward comments: "a parlor and bedroom, eh?" Then aloud to her brother's chum, in the rather patronizing style she allowed herself toward that youngster on account of her three or four years' seniority, she said, "Master Robert, I suppose this is all your taste?" glancing at the carpets and the furniture.

"Master Robert" inwardly writhed and outwardly smiled on this sweet-voiced personage.

"All my taste except two or three old things my uncle always will insist on having." Then, as Miss Stanhope was turning away, he exclaimed suddenly, perhaps to detain that fascinating yet most provoking young woman a little longer, — for poor Robbie was notoriously "spooney" on Frank's bright face and natural ways, — "Miss Stanhope, you 'll be sure to like my uncle; he 's the nicest old fellow in the world!"

"Oh, is he?" returned Frank, carelessly, and then she went on her way up to her room, to Rob Barker's great disappointment, doubtless.

"The nicest old fellow in the world!" she repeated to herself with a little shrug of her shoulders. And then she recalled her dream, and laughed. She could not but acknowledge, however, that this nicest old fellow's taste was not out of the way in the choice of pictures, when, coming down from her room one day at the end of the week, she lingered to look at two lovely landscapes that faced the open door. As she lingered there, she heard some one making frantic attempts with a latch-key outside,—attempts which proved futile, as a sudden ring at the bell gave evidence. Frank at this, ran swiftly down, and opening the door, said in explanation,—

"It 's that stupid new Biddy's work; she *will* slip the wrong bolt when she goes out."

It was Rob Barker's face that presented itself first to her, and that young gentleman found tongue to say at once glibly and politely,—

"Thank you, Miss Stanhope. But it was too bad to trouble you." And then, in another tone, "This is my uncle, Mr. Hadley; Miss Stanhope, Uncle Robert."

Frank looked at the new-comer, and saw, to her utter amazement, a man rather above the medium height, very square as to the shoulders, very broad as to the chest, very firmly knit together, yet with the lithe carriage such as one seldom sees beyond youth, and with a face that went well with all this, — a face bronzed and ruddy from travel and out-door life, yet intellectual and refined,— the face of an educated gentleman, and this gentleman clearly not a day over forty.

Frank thought of her dream; of the gray-headed, frosty-bearded old gentleman who had hitherto held peaceful possession of her mother's house; and of her mother's intention that only such should hold possession; and the thought was too much for her composure at the moment. She would have given much to have restrained that little irrelevant, and rather irreverent, laugh, but it was beyond her control. There was something so merry and natural in it, however, that it proved contagious, though it *was* irrelevant. Rob, in his "hobbledehoyhood" thought, "She's laughing at the mess I made with the latch-key." Mr. Hadley thought, "Nice, merry little girl;" and then they all went up-stairs together, and then Frank nearly burst out again, at her mother's look of astonishment when "Uncle Robert" was presented to her.

Aunt Tom, as they called Mrs. Alroyd, coming in that evening, Frank could not restrain her fun, and so the story of the new arrival was chronicled in such merry vein as only Frank was mistress of.

"Think, auntie, I fairly laughed in his face when I saw him, it was so funny to imagine mother's amazement and consternation."

Mrs. Stanhope looked excessively annoyed at Frank's merriment, and very soon managed to send her away on some household errand. The moment she was out of sight Mrs. Alroyd began: —

" Kate, I think you are perfectly morbid on that subject. The idea of your supposing that everybody will suspect you of matrimonial designs for

Frank and Ellen if you let your rooms to young lodgers."

"Mary, it is n't merely that — though that suspicion is a very common one, and one I do wish to avoid. But when we were girls don't you remember the Traceys?"

"Yes, what of them?"

"Well, you were younger than I, so you don't know, I dare say, what I knew. Mrs. Tracey rented her rooms to lodgers as I do. They were usually occupied by young men, and of course people were ill-natured enough to say constantly that her three girls were 'setting their caps,' and 'after' this one or that one. Those horrid phrases! But that was n't the worst of it. The Traceys were a good, old respectable family, not aristocratic by any means, any more than the Stanhopes. The rooms, however, were rented quite frequently to young men of fashion. It was very natural that pretty girls like May and Alice and Sara Tracey should be pleased by these elegant young men; should linger on the stairways talking with them; should accept bouquets and Christmas and birthday gifts from them; should, in short, with such opportunities, fall in love with such dazzling heroes, and expect to marry them. But, Mary, not one of these heroes offered himself in marriage to them. Not one of them went farther than those flirtations. They were simply passing away the time. It came in their way to talk, and now and then offer little attentions to these girls, and so the matter ended for them. But not so did it end for the girls. I happen to know that Sara Tracey almost broke her heart for Morris Ryder, and I know that May and Alice were more deeply interested in those young Stanleys than was well for their peace of mind. Then the remarks that were made were of course not agreeable. There is always something humiliating in the position of a woman, when she is so placed or so places herself that she can be flirted with, or approached as an acquaintance to talk and laugh with, without being sought. And any mother should shield her daughters from positions like these if she can."

" Well, I believe you are more than half right, Kate," Mrs. Alroyd replied in a tone of conviction. " I had never looked upon it so deeply before, I must confess. Not having girls of my own, you know, I 'm not so sensitive as you are."

" Well, I *am* sensitive, Mary, on this point. I would like as well as any mother to see my girls well married, but I don't mean they shall be what is called 'thrown' in any gentleman's way, nor stand a chance of being 'condescended to,' and all that sort of thing. We are poor, and not fashionable people by any means; but my girls are ladies, and I mean they shall hold themselves, and be held as such."

"How your mind does hold on to things, Kate. I should never have thought of making a personal application, or taking a warning from anything so far back as the affairs of the Traceys."

"Well, perhaps not. But I was older than you, and I never forgot that story."

"But, Kate, I don't believe you need trouble yourself about this Mr. Hadley. He is not a young man like Morris Ryder or the Stanleys. He won't be likely to flirt on the stairways with Kate or Ellen — a man of forty!" And Mrs. Alroyd laughed.

Mrs. Stanhope laughed, too, at this close application of the story of the Traceys; and so the conversation ended. But Mrs. Stanhope's thought on the subject did n't end with her words. She knew that this man of forty was one of the handsomest men she had chanced to see lately, and whose associations, if not his tastes, were with the fashionable world. And at this conclusion she said to herself: "But, perhaps, I 'm making an old fool of myself. I do hold on to anything so, as Mary says."

As time went on she began to think that she *had* been over-anxious, for nothing could be more satisfactory than the course of affairs. There were none of those stairway meetings and talkings she had such a horror of. Only a courteous and rather stately " good-morning " or " good-evening," occasionally, in a swift passage to and from the door.

" There never was such a proper and discreet bachelor, mother," Frank, who must always have her fun, commented to her mother. " He 's as grave and proper as one of the patriarchs."

In the mean time this " grave and proper " bachelor, who had learned the family circumstances from his nephew, was wishing he could be of service to his neighbors.

" That little girl who opened the door for us, and laughed in our faces, that first night, Rob, might do something with that voice of hers if she liked," Mr. Hadley said one evening, when Rob Barker had been holding forth on these family circumstances, which he had gathered from indiscreet Harry, who had divulged more of the pinch in domestic economy than he meant to, in his boyish talk of his own future help.

" You 've heard her sing ? " Rob remarked, questioningly.

" Oh yes. I often leave my door open, when I 'm in the house, to hear her. She really has a remarkable voice."

And just as he spoke there floated to them the wild sweet notes of an old German song which Mr. Hadley had listened to many a night upon the

Rhine. He listened now, smoking his after-dinner pipe slowly and thoughtfully. When it was ended, he knocked the ashes carefully out of the bowl of his meerschaum, and laying it down upon the corner of the shelf, rose up and proposed to Rob that they should go down into the parlor and ask the young lady if she would be kind enough to let them listen to her singing under more advantageous circumstances. " I dare say she sings a great many of those old German ballads, and there 's nothing I should like to hear so much."

Rob was, of course, delighted. They found the little family circle complete. Mrs. Stanhope plying her needle by the drop-light, Ellen, near her, going over some school compositions, and Harry putting his flute together preparatory to accompany Frank's playing. If Mrs. Stanhope was not pleased at this interruption she did not show her displeasure, and certainly she could have had no reason to have found fault with Mr. Hadley's manner. He was quite absorbed in the evident memories called up by the songs to which he listened. And after the singing he drifted into a little talk of German life, especially the musical life ; and as he had known many of the masters of the present day this little talk was very entertaining.

As he was bidding them good-night, with his cordial " thanks for Miss Stanhope's goodness," he smilingly, though quite in earnest, remarked : " It is n't exactly fair, Mrs. Stanhope, that your daughter should let only a few enjoy such a voice as hers. A church choir would find her invaluable."

Frank looked up eagerly.

" But, Mr. Hadley, my voice is n't trained at all. It knows as little of science as my fingers. I play and sing a great deal by ear, you know; though I *can* pick out my notes when Harry pushes me up with that remarkable flute of his ; " and she looked with one of her little grimaces at Harry.

" You 've heard so much good music, Miss Stanhope, that your voice is better trained than you imagine ; and I think you would find no difficulty in a choir."

This was a great word for Frank. " If I only *could* get a situation as soprano ! " she exclaimed, with inward exultation. Whereupon she fell to singing church-music with a will. Morning, noon, and night Mr. Hadley would hear that sweet voice ringing high and clear in anthem and choral. One evening he brought home with him a church organist — a real master of the great art. They sat talking together over their German experiences, when all at once a note ascended to them which stayed the words upon the musician's lips. A full, soft, clarion-clear note, which caught up and carried on a flow of silver song so pure and sweet, that even Mr. Hadley held his breath in a little surprise as he listened. As for his companion, he waited a moment as the voice ceased, and then, turning to his host, asked the question which that gentleman was expecting to hear, —

"Who owns that nightingale, pray?"

Mr. Hadley gave him the desired information; and then they talked animatedly for the next fifteen minutes about this nightingale. And then Mr. Hadley went down to Mrs. Stanhope's door, and asked if he might be allowed to bring a friend of his into her parlor to hear Miss Stanhope sing, if that young lady would be so kind. And Frank unwittingly sang to one of the greatest critics of the day — sang, as she said, without much skill, but with all her heart and her soul, and one of the richest, sweetest voices in the world. The strange gentleman, whose name they did n't hear, made but few comments, but his thanks were sincere, and his face a mirror of delight as he listened.

"Well, you were not disappointed, were you?" asked Mr. Hadley, as they once more sat alone together.

"Disappointed? No! She has a splendid voice. The very soprano we want. I thank you for your suggestion."

A few days following this Mr. Hadley was coming down from his rooms, when Mrs. Stanhope's parlor door was suddenly flung open, and Frank appeared upon the threshold.

"Oh, Mr. Hadley, I want to thank you!" she said brightly.

He smiled. "For what, Miss Stanhope?"

"For my situation as soprano at —— Church. I know it was through your suggestion that it came to me."

"My friend hardly needed a suggestion, Miss Stanhope, when he heard your voice," returned Mr. Hadley.

"But you *did* suggest it some way, I know, and I am very happy about it."

Mr. Hadley smiled again. "That is very pleasant for me to hear, Miss Stanhope. It's a great thing to be very happy; and I'm very glad if I have been instrumental in the smallest way in bringing about such a desirable result."

Frank laughed, there was such an indescribable air of humor in this little speech, and in the kind eyes that regarded her.

"I dare say you think that expression very exaggerated, Mr. Hadley, but I *am* very happy about this situation."

"I beg your pardon, Miss Stanhope, if I seemed to consider your expression exaggerated. Perhaps I did for a moment, because, as I say, it's a great thing to be very happy. But I see you are in ear-

nest, and I see, too, that it is a very natural thing
to be very happy over a situation like this."

He was quite grave and earnest now, and so entirely simple that Frank, who was so simple herself
and at home with everybody, returned, in honest
confidence, —

"Of course, I can't help but be very happy, Mr.
Hadley, to find myself all at once of so much help.
Why, I am to to have six hundred dollars a year;
as much as Ellen gets for her daily school-teaching.
And I have only to sing for it — just think of it!"
and she made such wide, bright eyes at this that
Mr. Hadley could n't help smiling again. She
laughed again at his smile.

"Oh, I dare say that seems a very small sum to
you, Mr. Hadley, but if you had spent your useful-
ness until now in sweeping and dusting and bed-
making for your board and clothes, and broken
your heart several times looking in at the shop
windows, I dare say it would seem a small fortune
to you."

"I dare say it would, Miss Stanhope," he answered, heartily, and laughing outright.

"Breaking her heart at the shop windows — the
child! I dare say she has," Mr. Hadley thought,
with a feeling made up of sympathy and amusement, as he went out.

Frank had said truly of herself when she de-

clared that she was very happy about this situation.
She was very happy to be of use, to help herself,
and to have the means of musical culture. She
went about the house singing her scales, or flinging
her voice out in some great rolling anthem day
after day; and Mr. Hadley used to hear the clear
notes breaking into his morning slumbers, or floating out over the house-tops like a lark's song,
as spring came and her attic window was opened to
the early sunshine.

Quite frequently now, too, he used to find his
way to Mrs. Stanhope's parlor when the sweet
voice was singing. Frank was so absorbed in her
music at this time, and indeed the interest between
them was so entirely musical, that Mrs. Stanhope
forgot her uneasiness and watchfulness for a while.

But if Mr. Hadley was interested in the music,
he was by no means unconscious that Miss Stanhope was a very pretty and charming girl. She
certainly did amuse him very much, and this fact
would have filled Mrs. Stanhope with dismay if she
had suspected it, for it was the very phrase she always applied to her old friends, the Traceys.
They amused people, and that was all. But Frank
went on her heedless, happy way, giving little
thought where she amused, but amusing herself
vastly. She had made the most of her opportunities and advantages, and risen so speedily into fa-

vor that in the early weeks of spring she was engaged to assist at a very *recherché* private concert.

"I am to sing 'Miriam's Song of Triumph,'" she said to Mr. Hadley, with that peculiar wide, bright-eyed pleasure in her expression.

"Do n't you feel a little nervous about it?" he asked curiously.

"No, I *had n't;* but do you think I ought?" she inquired archly.

"Not by any means!" he replied, laughing.

"Why should I feel nervous?" she said, more gravely; "the director says I have learned my part perfectly, and when I once get to singing I shall forget all the people around me; I always do."

If Mrs. Stanhope had glanced up from her work just then she would have seen an unmistakable look of thoughtful admiration on Mr. Hadley's face. But she did not lift her eyes from her darning, and Frank veered off from her gravity into her amusing vein.

"No, I 'm not nervous about the singing, but I am very nervous about my dress. I wanted a new pink silk, but mother said it was too showy for me; so I am coming out in an old blue crêpe, which was mother's, and I shall look like the ghost in Hamlet with my white lace and silver ornaments."

She laughed, but Mr. Hadley could see that she was a good deal in earnest; he had tact enough, however, to conceal both amusement and interest as he noticed her mother's reproving face, and caught the admonitory, "Don't, Frank!" But his artistic sense sympathized with her. Blue did not suit her white but not fair skin, her warm, hazel eyes, and chestnut hair. Pink would have made her dazzling. "Poor little girl!" he thought; "so the domestic economy will not yield a pink silk, even with the added six hundred dollars a year. Something ought to be done for her." And something was done.

"I told you I should look like the ghost," she said to her mother, as she came down stairs into the parlor the night of the concert.

Mrs. Stanhope was not quite satisfied herself.

"You might have my coral ornaments," she remarked, doubtfully.

"Oh, no! that opaque red against this blue would be dreadful!"

There came a knock at the door. Mrs. Stanhope said "Come in;" and Mr. Hadley entered with his hands full of the most beautiful roses — hot-house roses, of a soft blush pink in hue. He had timed it well.

"This is to exorcise the ghost, Miss Stanhope. There is nothing prettier, you know, than this deep blush-pink with that light blue. Is n't it what you call Pompadour?"

"Oh, Mr. Hadley, you 're like the Fairy Godmother! They are just the thing, and I thank you a thousand times." And, turning to the glass, with quick, deft fingers, she very soon metamorphosed herself into a glowing "phantom of delight." "Oh, how it does change all that pallid moonshine, does n't it?" she exclaimed. "It 's marvelous what effect the pink has on the blue! Is n't it lovely?" and she turned herself and her roses full upon him, with the innocent, one-thoughted question.

"Very lovely!" he answered, with more significance in glance and tone than he quite meant to show. The least little blush crept up into Frank's cheeks, and, matching her roses, made her lovelier than ever. Of course Mrs. Stanhope was anything but pleased at this little by-play. At once all her old fears sprang up, and beset her with anxious thoughts, while that old story of the Traceys began to haunt her like a warning ghost; and that evening, when she saw Mr. Hadley about a dozen seats from her talking gayly and animatedly to a party of aristocratic-looking girls, her mind reverted to Morris Ryder and the Stanleys. He belonged to the same world that they had belonged to; was wealthy, as they had been; and he would, probably, when he came to marry, choose a wife from his own peculiar circle, as they had chosen. If he was pleased with Frank's bright face and natural ways ; if he was interested in her music, and enjoyed her singing, it was much in the same manner that he was interested in a little German artiste of whom he spoke as " as an admirable young woman, who deserved encouragement." .

Thus Mrs. Stanhope argued ; with how much reason we shall see. While she was vexing her soul with these anxieties and suspicions Frank was pursuing her course, untroubled by any anxieties or suspicions. "Miriam's song of Triumph" was verily a song of triumph for herself; and Mrs. Stanhope seeing how happily occupied she was with her musical life took a little comfort thereby, and made no sign of her inward disquiet, though Mr. Hadley was not an infrequent visitor by this time. The bond of their mutual love of music was very favorable to acquaintance, and certainly this acquaintance did progress rapidly, and the conversation between the two was by no means confined to one topic, on the occasions of their interviews.

"Frank," began Mrs. Stanhope one day, in some trepidation lest she was making a mistake in speaking at all, — " Frank, do you think it quite wise to talk so much with Mr. Hadley, on all sorts of topics, in that intimate way ? "

Frank opened her eyes very wide. " For pity's

sake, mother, what *do* you mean by that ' intimate way ? ' "

" Why, my dear, I only mean that *natural way* of yours. You are not fast or free, but you are so at home with everybody that some persons might misunderstand it."

" Mother, Mr. Hadley has too much sense to misunderstand me ; and no man, unless he was a fool, could think I meant to make any more of our acquaintance than is apparent on the surface."

This was delivered with Frank's most vehement emphasis, and with a scarlet flush on her cheek. Mrs. Stanhope wisely forbore further remark on such a delicate subject, and so the days went on, and brought another day, when there was to be a great musical festival. Mr. Hadley, going up to his room one afternoon, picked up a long, fluttering scrap of pink silk, that floated down from an upper stairway. He smiled, and thought to himself, —

" So, the pink silk is achieved."

Entering his parlor, he went straight to a Japanese cabinet, where he kept choice gatherings from his European tour, and, unlocking it, brought forth from a little inner drawer a collection of cameos. From these he selected three, of a delicate pearly pink, — those loveliest and rarest of the cameo variety, — and laying them upon the strip of silk contemplated the effect with evident satisfaction. The cameos were without setting of any kind at this time — just the beautiful pink-white shell, cut by a most skillful hand. By the time the pink silk was completed these three cameos were shining resplendent in settings so cleverly imitating the antique that one would have pronounced them an heir-loom. Frank and her mother, sitting together in the parlor after tea one day, were not surprised to see Mr. Hadley make his appearance. He had quite got into the way of dropping in after tea.

"See how well I can match the pink silk," he began, smiling.

Frank looked up mystified; but he came nearer, and spreading out the scrap of pink silk upon her work-basket, laid upon it the choice pink cameos in their antique settings.

Frank's first exclamation was of delight as the effect struck her. Then that second sense crept on, and she glanced involuntarily at her mother. Mrs. Stanhope's face was overclouded by a very grave look.

"They are some of the thousand and one things I collected abroad, Mrs. Stanhope," Mr. Hadley remarked here, easily; "and when I picked up that scrap of silk the other day I thought the best use they could be put to would be to be worn as a match for that. They have been knocking about so much I see they are a little scratched; but if Miss Stanhope will wear them she will be more than welcome to them. for I am too heedless a fellow to like the care of such things."

He had been very diplomatic in his careless ease; but Mrs. Stanhope, who had lived her day, knew what a costly gift this was. She thought her answer would convey all she wished him to understand.

"You are very kind, Mr. Hadley," she said; "but, under the circumstances, I had rather Frank would n't receive so expensive a gift."

There was a grain of impulse in Robert Hadley's composition, which years and experience and a strong will had not quite overcome. It now and then betrayed him into swift speech. So now, in his surprise, or perhaps irritation, he exclaimed quickly : —

"What circumstances ?"

Brought to bay so directly, *she* thought so coolly, Mrs. Stanhope was a little indignant, and she answered, therefore, rather sharply and to the point : —

"You are comparatively a stranger to us, Mr. Hadley, and, at the most, our relation is but a business one, — at least it began so; and though you have been very kind and friendly to us, yet an acquaintance like this is different, and one feels differently about it, than one commenced through intimate friends."

"Oh, that's it, is it? I thought a friend was a friend under whatever circumstances you found him. But as you don't hold the same opinion, Mrs. Stanhope, I ought to beg your pardon for a great many liberties I've taken in the way of coming into your parlor uninvited, for, according to your view, I'm only a business acquaintance. Mrs. Stanhope, you're too bad!"

Mr. Hadley had begun this speech in rather a nettled tone and manner, but at the last he wound up suddenly with a quick, good-natured laugh that disarmed his listener more than anything else. She laughed in return, and retorted: —

"I think *you* are too bad, Mr. Hadley, to willfully refuse to understand me."

"But, you see, I'm not up to it, Mrs. Stanhope. I've lived abroad so long these American delicacies and hair-line distinctions are beyond me."

Mrs. Stanhope didn't believe a word of this; but it was useless to get into further discussion, so made no reply.

" And you won't consider me a friend and let that little girl take these trinkets then?" he asked, presently, under his new veil of humor.

" I had rather she did not, Mr. Hadley."

Mr. Hadley bent forward with a vexed look,

and gathering the cameos together crushed them recklessly into his pocket.

" You have made me feel like a great blundering boy, Mrs. Stanhope," he said, out of the quick, impulsive mood she had invoked.

His action was certainly boyish in a certain sense, but just as certainly not blundering or awkward. As he said this, and rose from his chair, there was such a grace and charm about him that Mrs. Stanhope felt that he was more than a match for her caution and watchfulness. She felt it still more as the days went by, and he made his " blunder," as he called it, a ground for still closer acquaintance ; for everybody knows that a laugh or a joke will break down more barriers and build up more edifices of friendliness than weeks of serious conversation. He was constantly alluding, when he met them, to the extent and quality of their acquaintance, as understood by Mrs. Stanhope ; and this in so gay and witty a manner that one could scarcely find fault with it. Frank grew easier than ever with him on this ground, for it suited her bright, audacious spirit. But Mrs. Stanhope was sorely perplexed. How would all this end? she perpetually asked herself.

In vain she tried to sound the extent of Frank's interest in this fascinating but most troublesome lodger. That young lady was either untouched, or carrying a high hand with her pride. She was quite capable of breaking her heart with laughing lips. That kind of nature always goes with her quality of high spirits.

In the mean time let it not be supposed that Miss Stanhope lacked attention or appreciation in other quarters. There was a young book-keeper in the firm of Alroyd and Dace whom her uncle and her mother especially favored. "He's a very promising fellow. I shouldn't be surprised if we made him one of us next year," commented Uncle Tom, with significance. Then there were sundry others — young men in responsible positions, or just entering business for themselves, who were very evident admirers of this sparkling, bright-faced Frank.

Mrs. Stanhope, coming in one evening from a lecture, found one of these admirers wearing a very rueful face, and her daughter looking a good deal confused and annoyed. Like a wise woman she asked no questions; but she was none the less certain that she had just lost a very worthy son-in-law; and with some irrelevance, but a great deal of impatience, she said to herself: " And it's all the fault of that Mr. Hadley. In love with him or not, Frank is getting spoiled for anybody else in seeing so much of him."

In this sentence Mrs. Stanhope fairly acknowledged the superiority, or at least the fascination of Mr. Hadley. But this acknowledgment was simply of externals and the accidents of position. Of the internal man she had no more or less respect than for any other man of the world. He was shrewd as they were; he was sensible as they were; he was generous as they were; he was selfish and fond of his ease as they were. This was the way she classed him — by generalities. And while she thus perplexed herself Frank and Mr. Hadley got on very pleasantly together. She sang for him, laughed and talked with him, and even got so far as to make her funny little grimaces at him upon occasions. But there was coming a change to all this. A series of small incidents, not very weighty in themselves one would think, brought this change about.

It was the first day of June, and Frank was putting the finishing touches to her toilet down stairs in her mother's parlor. She wore a white tarlatan, for she was to sing at a morning concert. A white tarlatan, with some puffings of illusion crusting it like foam. As she stood before the glass, fastening a knot of heath in her hair, she saw Mr. Hadley ascending the stairs.

" You are like a lily in all that white stuff," he said, coming forward into the room.

" I 'd rather be a rose — it suits me better; but

Harry forgot to go for my roses, so I pulled this heath out of a bouquet I had," she answered, absently, as she tried to get the heath into order.

"What time are you to be at the hall?" he asked, leaning against the piano in an idle, leisurely manner, as if time and its hurries were nothing to him.

"In about half an hour, if I ever get this rubbishy heath in."

And as she ejaculated this, in her little impatient way, she tore the rebellious spray out of its fastening and brought down with it two or three fluffy curls she had taken great pains with. Her cheeks flushed, and quick as her quick thought she flung the offending heath-spray impetuously upon the floor with a childish "There!"

Mrs. Stanhope said reprovingly, "Why, Frank!" But Mr. Hadley laughed, giving his head a certain backward movement that denoted with him great amusement, and then leisurely walked out of the room.

The half hour had not quite elapsed when he came back to find Frank tying on her white cloak, and still looking rather disturbed.

"I've got your roses," he said smilingly, uncovering a broad, deep basket where such treasures of rose-wealth lay, in hues of pink and white and blush, as to call out Frank's wildest admiration and most impulsive expressions.

"They are perfectly exquisite, perfectly; and you are just as kind as you can be to get them for me at this eleventh hour, Mr. Hadley."

Then she ran to the glass again, and in a happy excitement, which was an inspiration, showered herself with these June-darlings.

Turning to him again when all was completed, she put out her hand, and said in yet more earnest gratitude, —

"They are splendid, Mr. Hadley;" and then with a little willful, half-laughing glance at her mother, which he did not lose, "and *you* are splendid to bring them to me, and I thank you with all my heart."

He joined her laugh, but his eyes lighted with some inward fire as he looked upon her; and as he took the little gloveless hand she had put out to him in her impulse of thanks, he repeated in a soft tone as he regarded her rose-crowned loveliness, —

"'Queen rose of the rose-bud garden of girls.'"

In this moment he seemed to have forgotten the presence of Mrs. Stanhope; but the next instant her voice recalled him, and with a sudden color in his cheeks he relinquished the little hand and resumed his ordinary manner. But in a few minutes more the carriage was announced, and quite as a matter of course he attended her to it; but Mrs. Stanhope, who was standing at the window, saw him bend forward and say something in a low voice as he closed the carriage-door, which something sent the color of all her roses into Frank's cheeks. In the midst of Mrs. Stanhope's perplexity a new thought pierced like a ray of light.

" What if, after all " — she said aloud, turning from the window. And then she fell into silent musing as she watched Mr. Hadley down the street.

But the next two incidents put out this new light, and brought on a violent change in the programme.

Rob Barker was leaning over the piano, listening and looking devoutly as Frank sang for him. She sang a soft ballad she had sung in the morning, and the scent of the roses — Mr. Hadley's roses — hung round her still. Mr. Hadley himself, at a little distance, leaned back in his chair and observed the two — the singer and her devout listener, with keen attention; and over her busy knitting-needles Mrs. Stanhope observed Mr. Hadley.

Young Robert had come to a climax of his admiration that morning. All that white tarlatan and illusion and roses and the sweet voice singing

out of it, had been too much for him. As the
sweet voice ceased now, he began pouring out his
thanks in rather glowing words. In the midst of
these words Mr. Hadley's voice struck in like a
chill : —

"Rob, who was that I saw you with this morning ?"

Rob looked exceedingly annoyed as he answered,
"Miss Leyton, sir."

Mr. Hadley seemed to be very much interested
all at once.

"What, little Katy Leyton," he went on, "grown
up into that pretty girl?   Yes, I remember — she's
near your age — eighteen or thereabouts.   A pretty girl — a very pretty girl!   But her mother was
a great beauty and a famous belle; one of a famous
family, of which old Tom St. Clair was the chief
and head."

Frank had turned from the piano by this time.
She had not her mother's morbid sense; and it
must be allowed that Mrs. Stanhope's over-sensi-
tiveness amounted to morbidness sometimes.   And
not having this sense, she did not perceive the motive that her mother did in Mr. Hadley's words.
Indeed she perceived no motive at all.

But to Mrs. Stanhope this motive was patent.
It was keen displeasure at his nephew's evident
subjugation to Miss Stanhope's charms.   A dis-

pleasure which found vent and carried warning and reproof in the contrast of suitability in Katy Leyton's youth and high family. Mrs. Stanhope rode her high horse at this crisis. "It's the old story of the Traceys over again," she said to herself. "Frank is a pretty, interesting girl like that Miss Schaffner, the German artiste, but not to be thought of as an alliance with Mr. Hadley's nephew or Mr. Hadley himself." And back her mind went, gathering all the old items to add to this evidence. Many a remark or an action she might otherwise have forgotten now came up and assumed gigantic importance. She was the more disturbed by all this when she recalled the roses that had lately bloomed in Frank's cheeks on more than one occasion when Mr. Hadley was present.

"What shall I do?" she cried mentally, as she reviewed her trouble that night. The next day, when Harry came home with the great news that he had got his situation in the firm of Slido and Sayles, with a salary of fifteen hundred dollars a year, she straightway saw what she would do. She would give up her lodgers. With the united salaries of the three and the income of the five thousand dollars they could do nicely.

"Jubilate!" shouted Harry, when his mother proposed her plan. He felt very happy and very grand that he had helped to this. Even Ellen's calm, quiet eyes took a new light. " And we shall have the old parlors again, and the south and west rooms !" she remarked brightly.

" And not be mewed up in back chambers and attics any more ! " broke in Harry.

Frank was sitting at the piano when the conversation opened, touching the chords of an old chant. She did not whirl about in her usual quick fashion when she was interested or startled. She played through several bars, and then turned slowly, with the words, —

" Have you told the lodgers ? "

" All but Mr. Hadley," her mother answered, looking up involuntarily to see the effect of her words.

But Frank's face betrayed nothing if she felt anything. She said little, it was true; but Harry's voice was so industrious there was small chance for any other. And while he talked she turned to the piano, and commenced playing again. And as she played Mr. Hadley came in, and Mrs. Stanhope disclosed her new arrangement to him at once. For a moment he looked grave and thoughtful; then he spoke pleasantly and kindly, congratulating them on that to which they evidently looked forward as a desirable change. 'And then he laughed, and took rather a jocose tone upon his own special interest in the matter, declaring that

Mrs. Stanhope was turning him adrift in the most hard-hearted manner. And through it all the music of that old chant went wailing. Frank never turned from where she sat but for a nod of greeting and good-night, and his stay was very brief that evening.

But as he sat in his room quite late smoking he heard the weird and solemn music of chant and choral played softly and fitfully. Long after it ceased, and his pipe was out, he still sat by the open window in the June twilight lost in thought.

It was in the middle of the forenoon on the next day that Frank stood in Mr. Hadley's room dusting the elaborate carving of the old-fashioned mirror-frame. Working and singing away, she heard no sound, but was suddenly startled by Mr. Hadley's reflection in the mirror, as he crossed the threshold. He was in her thoughts, but she supposed him out of the house. The color rushed into her cheeks, and she put her hand to her head to pull off the white handkerchief with which she had covered her hair from the dust.

"Wait a minute!" he remonstrated. "You look like a quaint French peasant-girl that way."

She made a little grimace, spite of her embarrassment, and said saucily:—

"I had rather look like Miss Stanhope, any day. I've seen those great Normandy caps stuck on the

French nurses' heads at Newport, and I think they are anything but pretty." Whereupon she removed the handkerchief, and smoothed her ruffled hair with the prettiest of slim little hands.

"Yes," he returned, smiling, "I think I like Miss Stanhope better." Then his eyes wandered to the mirror and back again to rest upon the slim little hands. "So," he said, "these are the hands that have kept my shabby old mirror so bright and shining? I fancy a good deal about here is the brighter for your presence. But what am I to do if I am to lose it?"

As he proposed this sudden question he bent upon her a look so full of meaning that the color sprang redly to her cheek again. There was a pause, in which one heart was certainly beating very rapidly ; then he moved nearer to her, and in another, a graver, tone asked, —

"Frank, what is it your mother has against me?"

It was the first time he had ever called her Frank. This, and the rest of his sentence, surprised her out of her embarrassment.

"Against you!" she exclaimed. "What can you be thinking of? I am sure she has nothing against you."

"Yes, she has. I have noticed it on various occasions. On our first interview, I remember, she did not look upon me with favorable eyes by any means."

A dimple in Frank's left cheek began to discover itself, and the next minute made a little well of frolic, as she burst into a laugh. *She* remembered that first interview too.

"Well," exclaimed Mr. Hadley, joining in her laugh, "so I recollect, also, you laughed in my face at that first interview. Now, I insist on knowing what it all means."

"It does n't mean that my mother has anything against you individually, Mr. Hadley, I assure you."

"Oh, it 's collectively then ; that 's more encouraging."

Frank did not mean to tell the story of her mother's peculiar prejudice, but a little bantering, a few adroit questions, and the whole matter was very clear to Mr. Hadley's mental vision ; clearer perhaps than to Frank herself.

"Frank," he began, after this, "have *you* anything against me, collectively or individually?"

She laughed, then answered, half-shyly, — "No — nothing."

"You do not object to my years, then? You do not disapprove of me for an inmate of your house because I am too young a man? Frank, how is it; am I too old a man for you to become an inmate of *my* house? There 's an old place down by

Burton Beach that bears my name. I went and put it in order the other day, and my housekeeper asked me when I was going to bring my wife there. I could n't tell her then, and I cannot tell her now, or ever, Frank, unless *you* will be my wife, for I will have no other."

His voice had deepened into the most tender gravity as he uttered these last words. There was anxiety there too, for beyond a blush this proud little Frank, true daughter of her mother, had given no sign of her heart. But now all this was changed; and as she turned and let her eyes meet his, and as she put those slim little hands into his hands, he knew that he had no further cause for anxiety, for he knew that even as he loved her she had loved him. He took her in his arms then and kissed her; but a little later, bending her head back, he looked into those eloquent eyes, and said half reprovingly, half smilingly, —

"You proud little thing, to never give me any sign before."

And later yet, when he had his talk with Mrs. Stanhope, he said to that lady : —

"I think you must all have been blind, Mrs. Stanhope, not to have seen from the first that my interest was of the deepest nature. But you were bound, you know, by your prejudice," he added, mischievously, "to believe that I was the wolf in the sheep's clothing."

Mrs. Stanhope replied to this by speaking more at length on the whys and the wherefores of her "prejudice" than she had ever spoken before, except to her sister Alroyd.

He respected and understood her motives better than she had hoped.

"I see, I see," he answered seriously; "and I think you are nearer right than wrong after all, Mrs. Stanhope." Then he returned to his mischievous gayety again. "But you are right only collectively, Mrs. Stanhope. Individually you have proved yourself wrong — and a little morbid, too, or you would have seen what must have been so patent. Why, bless my soul, I believe I was even a little jealous of that boy Robert at one time."

Mrs. Stanhope smiled as she recalled her different interpretation of his feeling about "that boy Robert." And, smiling, she said to herself: "I believe we *were* all blind in this matter."

All blind, perhaps, but one. Cool and quiet and apparently unobserving, Ellen only evinced no surprise when it was told her that Mr. Hadley was to be her brother-in-law.

"I knew it was coming to that," she said smilingly; "I saw it from the first."

Mr. Alroyd, who always had to have his say, declared coolly that he had seen it from the first, too; but Frank, making one of her drollest grimaces, asked him why, then, he had been so anxious for her to smile upon that remarkable young book-keeper of his. And Uncle Alroyd, who never liked to be put in the wrong in any way, could only shrug his shoulders at this and declare that Frank was entirely too hasty in her conclusions.

6

A FOOLISH GIRL.

D ON'T stare so, Annie; it 's very rude of you."

"But she does n't take the least notice of me."

"Well, it 's rude to stare at any one so, all the same. Do come on faster, Annie. I 'm ashamed of you."

"Oh, but she interests me so much, Alice. While everybody is out of doors walking and talking, and listening to the band, she sits there alone and neither seems to listen nor to look at anything. Alice," in a softer voice, "do you know I think it is one of those French girls who has got bad news of her — her lover, perhaps, in the last mail. There are ever so many French families here from Paris."

Alice laughs; for Alice is matter-of-fact and unimaginative, and consequently does not invest every pretty, melancholy-looking face with a tragedy because there is a war going on at this time.

"Of course you 'd get up a romance, Annie. I dare say it 's only somebody who has a fit of indigestion. There, Uncle John is beckoning to us; we must go on now. · Come!"

A young man sauntering up the street, just arrived at this little Breton watering-place, which at this season is so full and so fashionable, overhears the conversation, and turns involuntarily to see the cause of it. If the fanciful little English girl could have seen his start of surprised recognition as his eyes rested upon the heroine of her romance, her "French girl" in the hotel balcony, she would at once have added another chapter to her romance. But if the girl, pale and dark-eyed, who sits there wrapped in a gray shawl, looks like a Frenchwoman, the young man who is now rapidly approaching her certainly does not look like a Frenchman, with his square shoulders, his stoutish build, and his close-cut reddish hair, and tawny, flowing beard. The prosaic Alice would no doubt have relished the utter demolition of her sister's romantic fancies if she had heard the unmistakable plain English of the hearty "How do you do, Miss Ada?" a moment later, and the response in the same accents from the "French girl." And when, in another moment, the gentleman repeats the bit of conversation he has just overheard, the laugh that falls readily from the young lady's lips dissipates entirely the supposition of a tragical love story in her case.

"The idea of my looking so sentimental as all that comes to, George!" she says, after her laugh.

"But you did look what our French friends would call uncommonly *triste*, when I first caught sight of you, Miss Ada."

"Did I? How interesting. If *triste* meant ill-tempered, it would suit the case very well. But come, tell me about yourself, George. You 're the last person I expected to see here. When I left New York you were in China, or some other outlandish place."

"And I have n't been home since. I sailed from there to England, and as I was a little worn out, I was ordered here."

Miss Payne regarded her companion for a moment with a little more attention than she had yet bestowed upon him. "You 've been ill?" she asked.

"Not exactly, but not quite well. I had too much care in Hong Kong. The book-keeper died there, and could n't be replaced for some months."

"Business, always business, with us Americans. It kills us." Then, with a short, unmirthful laugh, "It has nearly killed me already."

"You? what do you know of it, Miss Ada?"

"I? Oh, I 've been at the hardest kind of business, George. Your tea business in China is nothing to governessing."

" What sent you into that ? " asks Mr. King in a surprised tone.

" What sends most people to work — lack of money, Master George."

" But you came — I thought " — George flounders in confusion. He has not that ready wit which enables him to steer clear of dangerous facts.

" Yes, I came abroad with the Carneys by their invitation, but I came as the children's governess. I dare say any other girl under the sun would find nothing but enjoyment in these circumstances, but I am not any other girl ; I 'm Adelaide Payne, with the quickest temper, and the meanest pride, and the most cantankerous spirit that you 'll find anywhere."

George King laughed. All this to him was only Miss Ada's exaggerated nonsense. With him her " quick temper " was proper spirit, the " meanest' pride " was independence, and the " cantankerous spirit " sore sensitiveness. But then you must take into consideration that George was in love with this young woman. In love with her, though she had rejected him nearly two years ago. He had now apparently resigned himself to the post of friendship. This was n't so difficult a thing to do with Adelaide Payne as it might have been with another woman, for she was curiously free from that kind of vanity or sentimentalism which makes some women, most women, selfish egotists in such matters. Six weeks after George had received his *congé* from her she met him accidentally, and, greeting him without a shade of embarrassment, began talking to him about some of her plans; for Adelaide had always some new plan on foot. Ever since then, whenever they had chanced to be together, Adelaide always treated him in the same easy way of intimate friendship; and George liked it. But sitting there with him upon the balcony of the Breton hotel, after a year's absence, she does n't talk to him any more of her plans, and George wonders why not, and something flashes into his mind to account for this silence, which turns him giddy. What if — King is the most delicate fellow in the world with his friends; he never asks them questions; but now, for the first time in his life, he begins to pump.

"And if you hate governessing, Miss Ada, and are not happy here with the Carneys, have n't you some new plan?"

"Some new plan!" And Adelaide Payne laughs a little bitterly. "I don't wonder you talk of some new plan; for I 've done little else in my life but make plans. What absurd thing have n't I undertaken? As quick as I was out of school, and that was altogether too quick, I can tell you, I began to have these plans to get a little more money to buy the endless gloves and gowns and the rest of the gimcracks that women need. My goodness, George! why don't gowns and gloves and the rest of the things grow ready for our picking? Fancy, though, how we lovely creatures would scratch each other's eyes out, getting the best of each other!" George laughs, and Ada goes on. " I used to make yards and yards of tatting, and sell it to my mother's acquaintances, in those early school-days. I think they knew how hard up we were, and started me somehow on that little commercial track purposely. After that I tried my various small accomplishments in numerous ways, winding up with that inevitable conclusion for all single women of small means, or of no means at all — teaching. I dare say, I 'm ungrateful and undeserving. I don't defend myself, but now I'm quarreling with that. George, you may laugh, but, seriously and honestly, I am disgusted with myself. Any other girl would have settled into a respectable worker by this time, but I seem to fly out at everything; and it is because I am cantankerous, I suppose. If I go on like this — and I 'm likely to for aught I see — I shall bring up in the poor-house."

At this concluding sentence George's heart goes up like a feather, and he draws a long breath.

" What 's the matter, George? are your lungs affected?" asks Miss Payne.

" No, it 's my heart," answers George quite seriously.

" You don't say so ! The result of that overwork. Just as I said. Americans are always killing themselves with work. I 'm on the same road to destruction, only mine is fretting over the work; but it 's all the same, it 's the necessity."

" Miss Ada, I don't see why you don't get somebody to do your work for you. I — I " — and George looks like a fool and fidgets with his great crop of red beard — " I know one fellow who would be very glad to do it."

" George ! "

King nearly jumped from his chair.

" I don't blame you for taking me up in that way. I suppose any man might be expected to think a woman was flinging herself at his head, who had been going on as I have. But I did think you knew me better."

" Miss Ada, Miss Ada, I had n't such an idea. I had n't, on my honor. I knew you never thought of me but as your friend. You were speaking to me as a man might speak to another."

" I was n't ! " retorted Miss Ada. " I was speaking to you like the most foolish of women — fretting, complaining, when there was no earthly use in it."

" The reason I spoke as I did," poor George

went on explaining, " was because I could n't help wishing that I might serve you in the only way I could ; for I 've never forgotten what I said two years ago, Miss Ada."

A moment's silence, in which Miss Payne regards the downcast face of her companion with curious scrutiny. Then, quite in another key, she breaks out, —

" George, you may thank your stars you are not rich."

The young man looks up in amazement. " What do you mean ? " he asks.

" I mean that if you were rich I should be base enough to marry you."

" Ada ! " The light that was never on sea or land flashes over George King's face. Miss Payne looks a little frightened at the effect of her words.

" Don't mistake me, George," she hurried on. " I do not mean — George, if 1 loved you I would marry you to-morrow as you are."

King's face flushed and paled; but all the light went out of it.

" I 've said a horrid thing, I know — a selfish thing; but I 'm not so bad as I might be, for, George, if you were made of gold, I could n't marry you if I did n't *like* you."

George lifted up his head again with a quick motion. " Thank you for saying that, Miss Adelaide," he responded.

"I don't deserve any thanks; I owed so much to you, George."

"You don't owe me anything, Miss Ada," answers George in his kindest tone. There is a pause; presently : —

"Miss Ada, if you feel that way about — about money, you know, I don't see why you have n't found some one who — who " —

" Who was a gentleman as well as a rich man — is that what you mean?" asks Miss Payne, extricating George from his sentence with that straightforward celerity of hers.

"Yes, that 's what I mean, exactly," assents George.

A little ejaculation of impatience from Miss Payne, and then : —

" George, it is only in novels that the rich man appears in the nick of time — the rich man who is a decent sort of person, in the same class or rank with the young woman who wishes to dispose of herself. Miss Braddon manufactures that desirable *parti* with the greatest ease. Her heroines get into difficulties, that is, they find themselves poorer than church mice, with not an idea where their next pair of gloves is coming from, when up pops the inevitable rich man, who is just as inevitably a gentleman with whom almost any girl in her senses would be in love anyway. I don't know such rich men ; I know, instead, a little wizen-faced horror — a widower of sixty, who is *not* a gentleman. He sits in front of us at St. Michael's, and stares at me, the wretch! every Sunday. They say he 's rolling in wealth ; and he got it at some dirty business to which no gentleman would stoop. And I know another rich man, an old bachelor, who eats his dinner in his shirt-sleeves summer and winter, and who sits on his front door-step, which is opposite Aunt Ann's, in the same beastly fashion of demi-toilet. I believe both these specimens are millionaires, and I 'd rather risk the poor-house — good gracious, I 'd rather kill myself outright — than marry either of them ! "

"I should think so ! " ejaculated George King with emphasis. For a few moments there is silence between them. George breaks it by saying, —

" You put a morbid value upon money, I think, Miss Ada ? "

" George, you don't know what you 're talking about," begins Adelaide, vehemently. " If you had all your life felt the want of money as I have — if you had seen those you loved pinched and straitened day after day, with always a dread before you of perhaps greater pinching and straits, which you were powerless to alleviate — I wonder if you or any other man would n't put what you call a morbid value on money."

"Yes, I dare say I should," King answers, with a sympathetic tone in his voice.

And here, the young Carney girls coming in, the talk ends. They all know George King, and all like him, and standing about him ask a whirlwind of questions. A little Carney suddenly says, —

"Oh, why did n't you come before, Mr. King, so as to go back with us next week to America?"

"Next week?" asks George.

"Yes, next week, in the Calabria, papa said to-day when we were out driving."

Next week, when the Calabria sails, George King is one of the passengers.

"Thought you were ordered here for your health, King. Are n't you leaving rather soon?" asks Mr. Carney.

"Oh, one place is as good as another for that matter, sir. It 's the sea voyage that I need."

"Um — yes, sea voyages are excellent for some diseases. What was the trouble, King — something about the lungs?"

"No; something about the heart," George answers with great gravity.

"Oh," and Mr. Carney looks into George's face for a minute and then walks on. Meeting his wife, presently, he says, "Kitty, King is spooney on Adelaide, I 've found out."

"To be sure he is! that 's an old story."

"Oh, it is, eh? Why does n't he speak up then?"

"Speak up! my dear, are you blind not to see that George is hankering after the girl, and that she does n't care a button for him?"

"That 's it, eh? Well, she 'll go further and fare worse in my opinion."

"In my opinion, too; but it 's of no use to say anything to Adelaide, she 's so headstrong." But nevertheless Mrs. Carney did say something to Adelaide on this subject; and Adelaide met it with this declaration: "But I 'm not in love with George King, Mrs. Carney. I like him for a friend very much, but I don't love him."

"I suppose you 've got some romantic ideal in your head, Ada."

"I don't know about it 's being very romantic; but I suppose every girl has what you call an ideal; that is, she knows what kind of a man would attract her most."

"Did you ever see this man, Ada?"

"No, not exactly;" and Adelaide laughs a little and colors.

"And you never will!" cries Mrs. Carney triumphantly.

A pause ensues while Adelaide counts the stitches in a piece of worsted work she is setting up for Mrs. Carney. Presently Mrs. Carney breaks the pause: —

" What kind of a man is he, Adelaide ? "

" What man ? " asks Adelaide, looking up in astonishment.

" Why, this ideal of yours ? "

" Oh ! " with some impatience, and then in the " headstrong " way : —

" There 's one thing — he 's a real masculine man, a man's man. I hate women's men ! "

" Well, George King is a man's man, as you phrase it, I should think, though he does n't bluster round like that Major Roberts you girls used to think so much of."

Adelaide's face suddenly flushed a deep, painful red ; and Mrs. Carney, who is looking at her, turned away — enlightened. If Adelaide could have heard her thought ! " So it 's that disagreeable Roberts that keeps her from knowing a better man when she sees him ! "

The two were in Mrs. Carney's state-room all this time. When they went on deck, a few minutes later, a new acquaintance awaited them — a trifling circumstance enough on many, on most, occasions perhaps, but on this occasion it is destined to be au event which will mark with change the course of two lives at least. The day is lovely — a blue sky, a fresh soft breeze, and the waves dancing in the unclouded sunshine. Under such influences the sea invalids find their way to the deck, some for the first time. The Carneys are all in a little group together, and George King is with them because Adelaide is with them. He is just saying to Adelaide : —

" How fortunate it is for you that you are not seasick ; if you had been " — and here he stops abruptly, and Adelaide turns to see the cause. He is looking at some one or something away from her, with an expression of absorbed astonishment, and another expression, mixed up with the astonishment, which Adelaide cannot fathom. She follows the direction of his eyes, and sees — a pretty, pale girl, leaning on the arm of an elderly gentleman. The next thing, George says, absently, " Excuse me a moment," and starts off toward these new-comers. Presently Adelaide sees something else that sets her thinking — a sudden, vivid blush upon the pale face which makes it charming. After what seems to be the most cordial of greetings George comes running back and addresses himself to Mrs. Carney. Will she permit him to introduce her to some friends of his? They were very kind to him at Hong Kong last year, — American residents there like himself, — Mr. Maynard and his daughter. Mrs. Carney is " delighted " in her cordial way, and goes off with George, leaning on his arm. In a little while they all come back together to what Mrs. Carney calls the " Carney corner," and Adelaide is introduced to

"Mr. Maynard and his daughter." The pretty pale face brightens now and then into positive beauty, and Adelaide very soon perceives that Miss Maynard in health is probably a brilliant girl, both personally and mentally.

"I know you will like each other," George suddenly says in an undertone to Adelaide. "She is n't at her best now, on account of a long illness. They left Hong Kong last year for this reason. A few months after I heard that she had died at Florence. You can understand my more than amazement on seeing her just now. I believe for a moment I thought it was her ghost," and George laughs in an embarrassed sort of way which is new to him. Adelaide, who is usually the most unobservant person, probably because she is so occupied with those little plans of hers, takes note of this embarrassment, and of various other ways that are new to her, before the day is ended. Mrs. Carney has also been observant, which is not so unusual, and that night she comes into the state-room which Adelaide occupies with Belle Carney, her own small eldest daughter, who is fast asleep, as a little pitcher with very big ears should be — comes in to free her mind, to say in an injured sort of tone, —

"Adelaide, that girl is in love with George."

"And what about George, Mrs. Carney?" Adelaide asks with a touch of scorn.

“ Well — George acts queerly.”

“ I should think he did,” the touch of scorn deepening. “ My opinion is that George *has* been, if he is n’t now, as much in love with ‘that girl,’ as you call her, as she with him ; but evidently the course of true love did n’t run smoothly — Papa Maynard standing in the way, as a relentless parent perhaps,” and Adelaide repeats George’s little confidence about Miss Maynard’s illness, her leaving Hong Kong, and the news of her death, not forgetting George’s embarrassment at the end. “ You see, Mrs. Carney,” she concludes, “ that George only heard of her incidentally, which to my mind is the indication of the little hitch in the programme of his romance.”

“ You may be right, Adelaide ; but it ’s very surprising, the whole of it.”

“ Surprising ? Well, I don’t know ; George is like the rest of his sex, I suppose. He must be making love to somebody. But this pretty well upsets your theory of Master George’s devotion to your humble servant. You discover now how much that is worth — how easily he consoles himself.”

“ But if you ’ve always discouraged him, Ada — and in these two years, you know, with no hope of you, and this girl near at hand — why, it ’s perfectly natural ” —

“ Two years ! ” Adelaide repeats ; and then she

confides to Mrs. Carney, George's words to her at the little Breton watering-place : " *For I 've never forgotten what I said two years ago, Miss Ada.*"

" Well, I never ! " is Mrs. Carney's emphatic exclamation.

" Not that it makes any difference to me," Adelaide goes on. " It 's nothing to me, of course, to whom he makes love ; I 'm sure I don't want to have him running after me ; I 've none of that sort of vanity. But it does make one feel disappointed in human nature to see such uncertainty of purpose in a man."

" So it does, dear," declares Mrs. Carney, in sympathetic indignation.

" It was so weak of George to say what he did to me under the circumstances."

" Well, I dare say he believed it was the truth, Ada, *then.* Men are so queer about us women ! " Mrs. Carney replies, with an air of wisdom.

" Yes, he believed it until he suddenly saw the ghost of Miss Maynard, probably. Well, I don't care anything about it, I 'm sure. Yes, I do — I do care ! " Adelaide bursts out with that quick candor of hers, that honesty of heart which has always made her friends pardon every fault. " I do care ! George was my ideal of a friend ; he seemed like a rock to me, and I can't have that feeling any more, can I ? I 've lost my friend ; or

I never had him, I only had a fancy, that's the truth of it."

" My dear, Jack says "— Jack is Mr. Carney — " that we women are fools about men ; that we expect them to be heroes of romance all the time."

" I hate men, any how ! — disagreeable, disappointing creatures, you never know where to find 'em !" Adelaide suddenly snaps out.

Mrs. Carney laughs. " Not so bad as that, Ada, I hope ; but I think, myself, that women are more to be trusted."

The next minute she says good-night and goes straight to her own state-room, and repeats the entire conversation to Mr. Carney, who exasperates her by going off into shouts of merriment and making certain criticisms and prophecies, which he is informed by his wife are very wide of the mark, and shows that he knows very little of women and their peculiar natures ; whereat he laughs again, and provokingly remarks, " Well, we 'll see, Kitty — we 'll see."

The Calabria makes a speedy voyage and a pleasant one. Cloudless skies and soft breezes most of the time bring gay groups upon the deck. None seem to enjoy themselves more than the Carney party. Miss Maynard discovers both wit and humor ; her father is full of genial bonhomie ; and George comes out so strong as a brilliant talker that Adelaide, who has generally known him only as a listener, looks in amazement. But Adelaide does n't enjoy the party. Miss Maynard is too much for her. She confesses to herself that the young lady is cultivated and accomplished. "But all that talk about Hong Kong — I don't see what you can find interesting in it," she remarks to Mrs. Carney, when that lady comments on the delightfulness of this very talk. "I detest personal reminiscences; I always feel left out and lonesome when they are not *my* personal reminiscences; and I think they are in bad taste, too, in general society."

Mrs. Carney, who cannot help finding Miss Maynard charming, says something laughingly to Adelaide about being a dog in the manger. And Adelaide replies in great scorn : —

"I 'm not a dog in the manger. George may marry her to-morrow for what I care. He is n't my friend any more, as I told you. But Miss Maynard and I are antipathetic; I felt it from the first."

"But, Adelaide, you were so distant from the first."

"I never liked that kind of girl," pursues Adelaide, without taking any heed of Mrs. Carney's suggestion. And Mrs. Carney, as she turns away, says to herself, "Um, I don't know after all but

Jack may be right." But not to Jack does she confide this sudden going over to his opinion. She keeps it bravely to herself, though that is the dullest work always for Mrs. Carney, who has the keenest relish for " talking things over." She cannot, however, bring herself to face Jack's laugh, and the " I told you so " expression which she knows would dawn in his eyes at her confession. She consoles herself, however, for her silence by the observation which she takes from her new stand-point. And what does she see? She sees Adelaide a little apart, self-withdrawn and silent. She sees George more active than usual in all external ways. He talks a good deal with Miss Maynard and very little with Adelaide, which is quite unlike the old way of things; but this may be the result of circumstances. Adelaide certainly is not very approachable. Several times George has made little overtures which have been met with anything but encouragement. And there was Miss Maynard smiling and friendly, and with all that background of the Hong Kong life, so fresh in both their minds, the discussion of which was a matter of entertainment to everybody but Adelaide There was the invalidism of Miss Maynard, too, which would call out a hundred and one attentions. But underneath all this there was something else, some under-current which watchful Mrs.

Carney began to feel. George had recovered from his embarrassment ; he no longer acted "queerly." But what was it, what link in the past, in those Hong Kong days, made a present atmosphere of unacknowledged intimacy? Adelaide, sitting wrapped in her waterproof and her silence, feels this atmosphere very sensibly, feels it and rebels against it, all the while she is saying to herself perhaps, " George is n't my friend ; it 's nothing to me what he does."

But George makes one more venture of friendship. It is just as the journey comes to an end, and they are all about to separate. He leaves Miss Maynard to her father then, and resolutely attaches himself to Adelaide, attending her with his usual unobtrusive courtesy, until he seats her in the carriage.

" You 'll come and see us soon," says good-natured Mrs. Carney, leaning out of the window as the carriage drives away. And just as George is lifting his hat to them, another carriage whirls by, and Miss Maynard's voice cries out, shrill and gay : " At the Fifth Avenue ! remember, Mr. King."

"Hong Kong must be a good school for familiarity of manners, I should say," Adelaide remarks snappishly, drawing down her veil.

Mrs. Carney bethinks herself of Adelaide's old free-and-easiness in ordering George about, and says nothing; and Adelaide, fatuous young woman, congratulates herself as she goes up to her room that night that she has turned her back upon her *bête noire* — that forward Miss Maynard. But, alas for these self-congratulations! Before a month has transpired, Miss Maynard is a frequent visitor at Mrs. Carney's, Mrs. Carney having taken one of her great fancies for that young lady. So the old shipboard society meets again without a break, but with a variety which makes a great difference to Adelaide, for of this variety there is one man of whom we have heard before — the Major Roberts of Mrs. Carney's detestation. This gentleman has the kind of good looks that men's men, like Jack Carney, call " showy," and women, especially quite young women, speak of as " so fascinating ! " and " a Guy Livingston sort of man, you know." It is needless to dilate upon this gentleman's popularity in feminine circles. We all of us know how fascinating to the ordinary feminine fancy is the Guy Livingston type of man, or a faint resemblance to that type. Adelaide, it would appear from Mrs. Carney's hints, has long ago succumbed to this fascination, and it would appear also, from the nature of these hints, that she may have been in some sort a victim — one of those upon whom the king smiled but to ride away; and this is not far from the fact. Two or three years ago Adelaide had met Major Roberts, and been the recipient of his attentions until he had been ordered away on a foreign cruise. Perhaps before he sailed the girl had discovered that she was only one of Major Roberts's " friends." But this discovery seemed to cast no discredit upon Major Roberts in her estimation; to take nothing from the glamour with which he was invested. He had never committed himself. He had only looked now and then unfathomable things from his handsome dark eyes; had, in fact, just evaded decided responsible love-making, and thus cleverly contrived to leave himself entirely free from responsible intentions, without losing the admiration of the girl he so successfully " left behind him." If you had told Adelaide that she was in love with Major Roberts, she would have scouted the accusation indignantly, but she would color and her heart would beat in answering you. The truth of the matter was, no doubt, that she was in love with love, and Major Roberts, with his handsome figure, his fine eyes, and great splendid dark beard, seemed to represent her ideal, to embody her fancy; and now here he was back again from his two years' cruise. with a bronze tinge to his brilliant complexion, which enhanced his Guy Livingston style wonderfully; here he was back, " and at his old tricks again," said indignant Mrs. Carney, as she noted his *dévoué* attentions to Adelaide — "attentions which mean nothing, just nothing at all!" the little woman indignantly explained to her husband. What was her astonishment when her husband responded : —

"But I am not so sure of that, Kitty. When Roberts was hanging round two years ago he hadn't a dollar besides his pay, and now, my dear Mrs. Carney, Mr. Lothario has rather a nice fortune which his father left him last year."

"You don't say so!" exclaims Mrs. Carney; and then she goes on, "but how will that alter matters with such a selfish fellow?"

"Well, the selfish fellow can afford to please himself, Mrs. Carney."

Mrs. Carney was silent in meditation. If this was true, here was the very opportunity that Adelaide had always desired — the rich man whom she could love. But if it *was* true, what of Jack's little theory? and with a small spice of triumph she puts this question to Jack himself. But Jack only laughs and quotes, —

"There's many a slip;"

and so the conversation ends. But not so do Mrs. Carney's speculations and observations end. Keeping a sharp lookout, after her sociable fashion, she sees that "there is something in" Jack's idea, for she sees that Major Roberts's attentions to Adelaide at this time have a certain quality of earnestness that they have never had before. All this time there is George King coming and going, and Miss Maynard also a constant visitor. To Mrs. Carney, who had planned her own little programme, this was a game of cross purposes; yet even now she could not make Adelaide out. The girl did not seem to be conscious of a change in Major Roberts. Her manner to him was as it had been almost from the first of this second meeting — a queer union of gay excitement and irritability. Mrs. Carney, always a match-maker, wonders at this crisis if she had n't better have a little talk with Adelaide and enlighten her, perhaps; "for the girl, I believe, thinks he is fooling with her in the old fashion," she says to Jack. But Jack Carney replies, like the man of sense he is :—

"You just let things work their own way, little woman."

It would seem that others besides Jack Carney have noted and commented upon Major Roberts's earnestness in his present pursuit; for one day an old admirer of Adelaide's, meeting Mr. Carney, says: "So Roberts is going to range himself, eh, as our French friends would express it? going to marry the little Payne girl? Nice girl and a very nice thing for her; don't you think so?"

"Well, I don't know — I dare say it's a nice thing for Roberts."

"Oh, you don't like Roberts, eh?"

"Yes, I like Roberts well enough, but I don't think this ranging of his, as you call it, is a particularly nice thing for the little Payne girl."

The young man laughs and goes away to tell his friends that Jack Carney does n't think much of Roberts. About the time that this conversation is taking place Major Roberts is leaving the Carney mansion after rather a prolonged interview with Miss Payne. Mrs. Carney is on the *qui vive* up stairs; for did n't Major Roberts, on entering the library and finding her in possession, say to her with a significant smile that he should like to see Miss Payne alone and uninterrupted for a few moments, thus plainly indicating his errand and his own confidence in the result? But Adelaide does not immediately leave the library after Major Roberts's exit. Minute after minute goes by, until the little clock on the shelf has struck the half hour twice. Mrs. Carney can stand it no longer. Perhaps Ada is shy; perhaps she is afraid that Mr. Carney is up stairs; and so, fraudulently fortifying herself, Mrs. Carney goes down to the library.

"Well, Ada," she says gayly, "why did n't you come up and tell me the good news? I 've been waiting a whole hour for you!" Ada turns her face from the window. What a curious look there is upon it, and what a curious tone in her voice as she says :—

" I had nothing to tell, Mrs. Carney."

" Nothing to tell ! " and Mrs. Carney in a few unguarded sentences, in her usual reckless fashion, lets out her own little interview with Major Roberts and its significance to her.

Then Adelaide finds her tongue, and a red flush comes into her pale cheek at the same time.

" If Major Roberts advertises his confidence like this, then I am certainly justified in saying that Major Roberts made a mistake, and that I was not to be had. as he thought, for his asking."

" What ! you don't mean to say, Adelaide, that you have rejected Major Roberts ? "

" And why not, pray ?   Better men than Major Roberts have been rejected ! "

" But I thought — I supposed " —

" Yes, I know you thought, and everybody, Major Roberts included, thought that I should only be too happy to pick up the Sultan's handkerchief whenever he pleased to throw it; but you 're all mistaken."

" But, Adelaide, after our conversation " —

" I never said I liked Major Roberts, never ! " interrupted Adelaide, passion vibrating in her tones.

" I 'm not alluding to Major Roberts, particularly, now ; I was thinking of our conversations about money. Major Roberts, you know, has come into a fortune lately."

"Yes, I know, but I never meant that I could marry a man without loving him, and I don't love Major Roberts — I don't like him, even, now. I did think once, two or three years ago — well, I did think that I was — that he was a sort of hero. But since I've seen him this time I've found out my mistake. Oh, Mrs. Carney, I've been such a fool! Girls *are* such fools! To think I should have admired him. He is so vain, so — artificial! not a man's man at all, as I thought him."

" Well, I'm glad you've found him out, Ada. I never could understand how you girls could be so deceived by that grand manner. But I must say I think you've been playing rather fast and loose, Ada, for you've certainly encouraged Major Roberts until everybody thought there'd be but one end to the matter."

"I have n't encouraged him, Mrs. Carney; I never thought he meant anything serious until to-day."

"What in the world *could* you be thinking of, then? Everybody else had seen how in earnest he was."

"Have they? well, much good may it do them," Adelaide replies irritably.

Mrs. Carney is certainly an amiable woman.

She looks a moment at Adelaide, as if turning over something in her mind, and then, instead of keeping up the irritating subject, says kindly : —

"Come out for a drive with me, Ada ; it will do you good."

It is a lovely day, the air full of warmth and brightness, and not a cloud to be seen in the April sky. So sweet is the influence of all this warmth and brightness, this tender atmosphere, that Adelaide's vexed spirit yields to it involuntarily, and something of a girl's hope and lightness comes into her heart and shines out upon her face at last.

"It really has done you good, Ada. I have n't seen you looking like . this for a long time," says Mrs. Carney, pleasantly exultant over the effect of her prescription. They are just returning to the city as Mrs. Carney says this, and Adelaide is on the point of responding, of confessing how much good she has gained, when a shrill, clear voice cries out : —

"Oh, Mrs. Carney, Miss Payne, how do you do? Won't you come in ? "

Adelaide turns her head in the direction from whence the voice proceeds, and sees Miss Maynard leaning over the gate, which shuts in a pretty green lawn, and at her side stands George King. The coachman is ordered to pull up for a moment — just long enough for Mrs. Carney to ask about the

new house, and if Mr. Maynard likes to be so far
out — if they have got settled yet, etc.; and then
Miss Maynard, as they move off, says in a quick,
happy way : —

"I am coming to see you very soon, Mrs. Carney,— to see you and to bring you a piece of
news;" and as she speaks she moves her hand to
her face. Perhaps it is to hide the rising blush in
her cheeks, but at the moment there shines and
sparkles out to them a ray of light and fire from
a solitaire diamond.

"A great, impudent diamond, Jack," is Mrs.
Carney's curious description, as she tells her story
of the day to her husband that evening. "And she
looked so detestably happy, Jack, I could n't bear
her!" Jack laughs, as he always does, at Mrs.
Carney's queer little turns, and puts her in a corner by saying : —

"'Thought you were a great friend of Mary Maynard's, Kitty ?"

"I like Mary Maynard very well, but I always
had a feeling that she had laid herself out to catch
George, and I hate that kind of girl," is Mrs. Carney's contradictory reply.

"I see — you had made a new plan to marry
George and Adelaide, the moment you found out
she 'd given Roberts the go-by; and Mary Maynard has upset this plan; and you know, Kate,

nothing ever vexes you like the upsetting of any of your little beneficent plans for other people's felicity."

" Well, Jack, there 's one thing : if your little theory " — What more Mrs. Carney would have said will never be known, for at this point a servant interrupts her with the message that Miss Maynard and Mr. King are down stairs.

" Did they ask for Miss Payne, Ann ? "

" Yes 'm, and I spoke to her as I came along, but she says she 's a headache and will be excused, if you please."

" Where is she, Ann ? "

" In the school-room, ma'am."

The school-room, as it is called, where Adelaide teaches the little Carneys, is at the extreme end of the house. It is a large room, cheerful enough when the sunshine is pouring in at the southwest windows, but looking very dismal as Adelaide sits there by a single low light, and a little chilly fire in a wide grate. But it has the virtue of being out of the way of everybody and everybody's noise, and thus a very fitting place for a person suffering with headache. Yet even at this isolated distance, Adelaide can catch now and then a faint, far sound of laughter from the drawing-room. In vain she tries to fix her mind upon Miss Thackeray's pretty story of " Elizabeth," which she has brought up from the

library; for it seems she does not find her headache so severe as to exclude her from reading, or
at least an attempt at it. But it is merely an attempt, not on account of the headache, but on account of her wandering thoughts. The Caroline
Gilmore of Miss Thackeray's story turns into Miss
Maynard as she reads — Miss Maynard, who has
taken her friend away. John Dampier gets mixed
up with George King and Major Roberts, and
Elly, poor Elly, — for she is in the midst of Elly's
troubles, — poor Elly suggests her own forlornness;
only Elly's case is nothing so bad as hers, as the
saddest of written stories seem tame to our own
stories when we are living them. By and by, over
the laughter, there comes a sound of music; there
are the gay notes of the piano, and somebody is
singing. It is Miss Maynard's far-reaching soprano,
which her admirers have likened to Parepa's dulcet
tones. But Adelaide shivers as she listens. She
has never liked Miss Maynard, and she hears no
sweetness in her voice. She makes another attempt to follow the story of " Elizabeth " instead
of her own. She turns the page and begins to
read of Elly's good friend, Miss Dampier, and
straightway her thought flies back to herself as she
thinks of Miss Dampier's sympathy and her own
desolation. If only she had such a wise friend!
Mrs. Carney is kind, but not like that sweet,

motherly Miss Dampier, to whom poor Elly could confess everything — all her foolishness and sorrow. Just at this point in her comparison a door opens somewhere in the upper hall, and the words of Hatton's pretty ballad, " Good-by, sweetheart," comes up to her full and clear, in Miss Maynard's clear voice. The next instant the song is shut out again, but somebody is coming down the long corridor leading to the school-room. It is very unkind of Mrs. Carney to send for her, Adelaide thinks, as the footsteps draw nearer, and some one knocks for admission. But that is not a servant who enters at her " Come in." She looks up quickly, and sees — George King. A little flush of angry surprise rises into Adelaide's face, which deepens as George speaks : —

" Mrs. Carney sends me up to tell you Miss Maynard's news, Miss Ada."

Adelaide can find no words to reply, and George goes on. He is telling her rather a long story, she thinks, about Miss Maynard, and Hong Kong, and a young German, whom Mr. Maynard did n't like. It is all very queer and confusing to Adelaide — she can't follow half of it, until at the end George says, with a laugh : —

" But it is all right now. Von Raden has been promoted for his gallant conduct in the war, and Mr. Maynard can hold out no longer."

"Von Raden? what has he to do with Miss Maynard?" asks Adelaide, bewildered.

George laughs outright.

"Well, I always knew I was a bad hand at telling a story. Von Raden, Miss Ada, is the lover of the piece."

"And you, George?"

"And I, Miss Ada, am the faithful friend of all parties — of Von Raden especially, who is an exceedingly good fellow, in spite of Mr. Maynard's prejudices against a foreigner. He will be here in the next steamer, Miss Ada, and then you will have a chance of seeing a very handsome young officer of the Prussian army."

"George, was it this secret about the Prussian officer which made you and Miss Maynard blush and look so queerly when you met on board the Calabria?"

George blushes again at this question; but he laughs at the same time, while he answers : —

"No, it was n't the secret about the Prussian officer; it was because Mr. Maynard had taken it into his head that I was a safer man than the Prussian."

"He wanted you to marry his daughter!"

"He did n't want her to marry the Prussian, Miss Ada," George replies modestly. "And it was n't until Miss Maynard gave me her entire confidence about the Prussian — which she did on the Calabria — that we were either of us quite free from embarrassment when we met, for we had both been made aware of Mr. Maynard's little plans in regard to us."

"And I thought it was you who were Miss Maynard's lover all this time, and I hated her, George!" cried Adelaide, with sudden, reckless impulse.

George is leaning against the mantel, but at this he starts forward and looks eagerly into Adelaide's face.

"Thought it was I, Miss Ada?"

" And I hated her, George!" Adelaide repeats irrelevantly.

Down goes George on one knee beside the little low chair that he may get a better view of the occupant. "Adelaide, do you mean," he begins; and Adelaide, with a great bright flush coloring her cheeks, answers honestly: —

" Yes, George, I mean that I hated Mary Maynard for — for your sake. I mean that I've been a fool, George, all these years. I mean that I was so used to having you for my friend that I did n't know, until I thought that Mary Maynard was taking my friend away, that " But Adelaide's vehement confession has spent itself, and the rest of the sentence is inarticulate upon George's coat collar, and with George's arm about her; and George is quite content to ask no further questions at that moment, for he has got his heart's desire.

"So you were right in your little theory, after all, Jack." Jack gives rather a sleepy yawn; and no wonder, for Mrs. Carney, just returned from a midnight interview with Adelaide, has awakened him from his first sleep to tell him her great news.

"My little theory?" he mutters sleepily. "Oh, that Adelaide is in love with King. I thought that was settled some time ago. I thought it was King you was n't sure of — I thought" —

"Jack, you 're talking in your sleep. Did n't you hear me tell you that it 's all settled between Ada and George?"

"Is it? Well, I am very glad something is settled for that foolish girl you and King are so fond of;" and with these words Jack Carney turns his face to the wall and goes back to the dreams that Mrs. Carney has so ruthlessly interrupted.

In the days that follow, while there is much rejoicing in the house of Carney over this foolish girl, the dear, discerning world, with its usual sagacity, hits the nail on the head in this wise: —

So Adelaide Payne is going to marry a poor

man, after all.   Such grasping ambition as hers always ends in this way.   She tried to catch Major
Roberts, you know, and did n't succeed, poor thing!
so now she takes up with that red-headed George
King.

OUR ICE MAN.

I.

WE are sitting on the piazza of the Ditworths' "cottage" at Newport. It is the summer of 1873, or rather the beginning of autumn, for it is just turned September. We are six in number: Mrs. Ditworth, her son Tenicke, Colonel Chadwick, my mother, and her two daughters, Rachel and Letitia. It is in the morning, just after breakfast, and we are sitting dawdling, digesting our breakfast and yesterday's news dribbled out to us by the Colonel and Tenicke; for, as is the custom in households with masculine members, the men of the party have at once appropriated the newspapers.

I am listening vaguely to Tenicke's voice running along in a jerky account of some races somewhere, in which I have n't the faintest interest, and catching Colonel Chadwick's exclamations of " By Jove!" and "What a set of fools now!" and "I knew the mare would win!" and I am thinking vaguely that it must be nearly time to drive to the beach, when Letitia breaks in, saying in one of her rapturous tones, " *What* a handsome fellow!" Letitia is always breaking into little fervors of feeling or imitations of feeling over somebody, always picking out charms unseen by other eyes; so I am not interested or moved by this exclamation. But the gentlemen of our party are not so stolid as I am. Letitia is n't *their* sister, and what she thinks of one of their sex is by no means an uninteresting matter to them. Tenicke stops his jerky reading and throws up his chin in that near-sighted way of his, and Colonel Chadwick wheels entirely about to follow the direction of Letitia's dark eyes; but both he and Tenicke fail to perceive the object of Letty's admiration. I laugh silently behind my fan, for I know the bent of my sister's mind. I know that she makes great pretensions toward being democratic in her tastes, and that she delights to astonish her fine friends by breaking out into what she calls honest admiration for a coal-heaver or some grimy giant of that ilk; and so, while Tenicke and Colonel Chadwick are entirely adrift and perceive no earthly object whereupon to waste that enthusiastic exclamation, I am perfectly aware that the great hulking fellow who has just disappeared up the carriage drive at our right — in short, our ice man — is the object of Miss Letty's present approval. "Blest if I can see anybody," says Tenicke after a moment.

"Must have been a hero of your dreams," says the Colonel, laughing feebly.

"Hush, here he comes again ; " and Miss Letty nods her beautifully gotten-up head to the right. "Oh, that fellah !" and Tenicke looks relieved. "Yes, very good-looking, — put together well. Looks as if he 'd pull a good oar if he knew how."

Chadwick yawns and says nothing. This "fellah" is out of the pale of his masculine jealousy, for Colonel Chadwick is put together well, and knows how to pull a good oar, and is something else besides — a great deal else, he thinks. So it happens that Letty's little remark falls flat and the races start up again. But we are not to be rid of Letty's ice man quite so easily. Presently there he is again, and, as if our talk had mesmerized him, his face is turned fully toward us with a look of curiosity in his gaze, which Letty at once translates into a look of admiration for herself. Then a sudden second thought assails her, and with that innocent air of hers, as if she had entirely forgotten her first exclamation of admiration, she says : "How like he is to you, Mr. Ditworth — how very like !" Then immediately she recollects, and calls up with that surprising will-power, one of those small blushes, and a pretty little air of confusion.

Tenicke smiles broadly, not displeased, and says, "Thanks, Miss Letty." Whereat I laugh, a discordant, disagreeable laugh, I am perfectly well aware, for nothing sets my teeth on edge like these little *minauderies* of Letty's, and Tenicke's pleased acceptance of them. Letty flings herself at his head, as she flings herself at every man's head; and he likes it, as they all like it. At my laugh he turns quickly and flushes. Then with a half smile, " You don't agree with your sister, Miss Rachel ? "

"I — what about, Mr. Ditworth ? " I make answer with malicious assumed oblivion. He knows it is assumed, and he flushes still deeper.

" Now, Ray, that is so like you — to pretend not to know of what we were speaking, to pretend that you did n't see the most striking resemblance between Mr. Ditworth and the — the ice man who just passed," says my sister.

I do not reply to the first part of this speech, but I stoutly maintain that I saw no possible resemblance to Mr. Ditworth in the handsome fellow of Letty's sudden admiration. But all the time I am going flatly against the truth; for even before Letty had spoken I had been struck with the curiously close resemblance, not merely of form but of feature, and something too of expression. But to feed Tenicke's vanity, to let him think for a moment that I was following in Letty's shameless

wake! Never. I would perjure myself fifty times
over before I would hazard the slightest suspicion of
that. In the mean time Colonel Chadwick is saying,

"Not such a bad-looking fellow really, but what
a dog's life to lead."

"A happy dog, I dare say," returns Tenicke.

The Colonel shrugs his shoulders and quotes
"If ignorance is bliss."

"I don't see why you need take it for granted
that only the idlers have any use for brains," I say
satirically. "On the contrary, as far as my knowledge of history goes, the great men, the brainy
people, always come up from the workers." Then
I quote freely, as far as my memory will allow
me, the great names that have shone on the world
unaided by birth and fortune. Tenicke smiles
again, one of those easy exasperating smiles of his,
and sitting back lazily in his chair he says :—

"I take nothing for granted, Miss Rachel, and I
dare say this son of the soil, to put it sentimentally,
may be carrying a volume of Homer in his pocket
while he carries his icy burdens; or perhaps he
may be studying some of the sciences in his leisure
moments, for I suppose he does have leisure moments. Perhaps he is a great geologist or a second
Tyndall in embryo ; and, regarding those blocks of
ice, he may be studying new forms of water."

I am in an inward flame, but outwardly I am as

icy as the subject under discussion, and I manage to hum in an absent way a bar of a Strauss waltz to show Mr. Ditworth that his impertinent familiarity in chaffing me is unheeded.

It is just here Letty says sweetly, "Oh no, not Homer, Mr. Ditworth, but *very* likely one of Bret Harte's books."

Mr. Ditworth rouses himself. "Miss Letty, don't you know that it is an established fact that Bret Harte is only appreciated by the people of culture or with the cultivated instincts, never by the class he writes about, unless it may be the John Oakhursts?"

"But this is a possible Tyndall, you admit, Mr. Ditworth, and consequently he *may* have the instincts of culture and be able to appreciate your Bret Harte," I suddenly say, forgetting for the moment my rôle of indifference and abstraction.

"Oh yes; I will concede to the possible Tyndall, Miss Rachel, with a low laugh and a quick glance shot at me. And here again down the carriage drive he passes, this possible Tyndall, this bone of our contention. As I catch a full view of his face and see the straight brows, the square chin, and above all the level look of the eyes that seem to look into mine, I have a sudden odd sensation that something queer is going to happen, not then and there, but somewhere and *some-when*, not far distant.

Tenicke, who had also been observing the man, suddenly drops into seriousness. "I dare say that fellow enjoys himself better than I do. He gets good wages, lives simply and heartily — no chance of his being bored, no chance of his making any great mistakes, no great risks possible to him. I 'm not sure but I 'd change places with him if I could."

"Oh, now, Mr. Ditworth, you know you would n't!" bursts forth Letty.

"Well, no, I don't suppose I would; but I stick to it a man might do worse. I 'm not sure but Miss Rachel thinks we are all doing worse, such fellows as Chadwick and I, dawdling round here."

"I think nothing of the kind, for I have no *thought* upon the matter," I reply lazily.

"It is eleven o'clock, and if we are going to the beach it is high time," remarks Mrs. Ditworth, rousing from a close conference with my mother upon the iniquities of servants and other domestic topics. I have no idea that either of them has heard a word of the conversation just narrated; but I am no sooner in my room than my mother's very sweet voice says, at my elbow : —

"Rachel, I can't think why you are so rude to Mr. Ditworth."

"Rude? I did not mean to be rude, mother; and I 'm sure if you could see Mr. Ditworth as I do, if you could understand all his superciliousness, his idle affectations " —

" Rachel, you are usually clear-sighted, but I think you are strangely blinded in regard to Mr. Ditworth. I have watched him very closely, but I see nothing, nothing at all of what you say : on the contrary, he seems to me to be very tolerant and kind to *you*, Rachel, who are anything but kind to him."

" Well, I 'm sure he does n't suffer for kindness. Letty fully makes up to him for anybody's cruelty," I retort rather flippantly, glad to find firm standing ground. But my mother does n't seem to think it firm standing ground.

" Letty is polite to every one," she says, with a slight frown.

I am exasperated, and unwisely, undutifully, perhaps, burst out, " Mother, you must see that Letty flings herself at his head."

" Rachel, how *can* you use such slang? How can you accuse your sister of such things ? "

" Because it is true," I say doggedly, " and Letty in her heart knows that it is true, and Tenicke knows that it is true ; and it makes me hate him, the cool, easy way in which he takes it — and likes it."

" Rachel " — there is a note in my mother's voice that brings me up sharply — " Rachel, if this

is all true, I don't see why you have such special
feeling about it. Letty, it may be, is unduly fond
of admiration, and strives to please; but it is her
way with every one, and — I never saw you so bitter about it before, Rachel."

I am in a flame, and I answer hotly, "I hate to
see her make such a fool of Tenicke Ditworth —
that's all. He's vain and idle and *blasé* enough,
heaven knows, but he was Jack's friend, and I hate
to see him made such a fool of."

" Letty isn't making such a fool, as you call it,
of Mr. Ditworth. I think he understands her better than you do, Rachel ; and if he likes one of
my daughters I am sure I shall not quarrel with
him for it. But — there is the carriage; don't
keep them waiting, my dear."

I turn to the window. My cheeks, which were
flaming a moment ago, feel stone cold. All my
hot anger has gone out and left me. I hear my
mother's steps going slowly down the stairs. I
hear her saying presently, " Rachel will be here in
a moment." But I am hearing at the same time
her significant words, "If he likes one of my
daughters I am sure I shall not quarrel with
him." Am I quarreling with him because he
likes Letty? This is what my mother thinks. I
forget for a few seconds the carriage that is waiting, forget everything in recalling all my mother's

words, all my mother's meaning; and as I recall, every one of them pierces me like so many arrows; and how cheap and mean and pitiful all my life seems, and how the color and brightness goes out of everything; it is then I suddenly hear, " What in the world keeps Rachel so long? " in Letty's clear tones. I arouse myself, and looking down I see Tenicke sitting in the high beach wagon, and I meet his eyes, and know that he has been silently observant of me all this while. I turn swiftly and run down the stairs, and in another moment am seated beside Colonel Chadwick on the back seat, and we are whirling along the avenue.

" What *did* keep you so long, Ray? " asks Letty. She is in the front with Tenicke, looking round at me curiously and noting my pale cheeks and my lacklustre eyes.

" I could n't find my hat," I lie boldly and briefly; and then all at once Tenicke asks Letty a question, and she forgets my existence. We drive on through the long English-looking lanes, sweet with fresh-mown lawns and the standing clover in the upland fields, and cool with the coolness that the close unseen sea brings. I hear as we go the chirr of the grasshopper, the whistling, calling, cooing notes of the robins, and the swiff, swiff of the lawn mowers, all blended together in a sweet summer sound, which will not shut out the sound of my mother's words, and Letty's careless chatter and light, happy, conscious laugh.

The tide is very high that day, for there has been a storm, and Letty, who has always a horror of the sea, hears some one say that the undertow is dangerous, and straightway falls into a little panic of terror.

" I *cannot* go in to-day. I know I should bring on one of my palpitations," she says in answer to Colonel Chadwick's remark that there is no possible danger.

Tenicke does not urge her ; on the contrary, he says with a queer shyness, " Don't urge her, Chadwick. Let her do as she chooses." Then to Letty, with a little eager hesitation new to him, and as if he were speaking to a child, " I would n't have you go in, Letty, if you feel like that : I 'm sure it would harm you."

A flattered look in Letty's eyes, a soft pink blush, a real honest blush, on her peachy cheek, at this ; and I turn away with my mother's words ringing through my brain. When I emerge from the bathhouse I see only Tenicke at my door. Colonel Chadwick is chatting in the beach wagon with Letty.

" I 'm afraid of the undertow," he says, throwing a laughing look at us, a look that seems to embarrass Tenicke, but which only calls out another fine little blush on Letty's cheek. All is fish that comes to Letty's net, and she never ceases to feel triumphant at any indications of a nibble.

So it happens that I go in alone that day with Tenicke Ditworth. I can see everything as I saw it then. The brilliance of the sky, the wonderful clear atmosphere that showed far off to us an ocean steamer on the blue horizon line, and the great vexed waves that still remembered yesterday's rage and wrath. The water, with all the warm sun, is chilly, and I shiver as it breaks over me.

"You are cold," says Tenicke. "Perhaps you had better not stay."

"It will be over in a moment, this first little chill," I return. As we breast the great waves and beat back the strong tide my words are verified. The chill goes, and the keen sense of exhilaration comes back to me. But the undertow that Letty was afraid of is a reality of which we have need to be careful, if we do not fear it. I turn for an instant to look at the steamer far out at sea, and the next instant have lost control of myself. It is then that Tenicke flings his arm about me and says, "Give me your other hand." His tone is imperative, but I do not quarrel with it. The need I very well know is imperative; and if it were less, if it were not at all, I did not care then. I had forgotten my mother's words ; I had forgotten his parting glance at Letty, his solicitous words to her, and what all these had meant to me. I forgot everything but just the moment — a wild, blind, intoxicating moment, in which I was alone out of the whole world with Jack's friend — Jack's friend : not the idle, *blasé*, supercilious gentleman I had sneered at for three weeks and more, had flung all my small shot of sarcasm at with a fierceness that had aroused my astute mother's suspicion and covered me with shame an hour before — Jack's friend; *only* Jack's friend, I lied to myself even then : even then, with his arm about me, with my heart beating wildly against his — even then and after as we floated out together, my hand still unrelinquished, and myself caught now and again in that swift embrace as the tide beat upward in its reverse current, threatening overthrow and danger ! Oh, how the beautiful day shone fairer than any day since Jack had died out of my days ! How the rain-washed heaven smiled with new cheer, and the sun warmed me through and through with its friendly beams ! As we go out, just up from the surf line we meet the beach wagon, and there is Letty smiling at us, or at Tenicke, who does not see her.

" Were n't you frozen ? " she asks.

" At first, yes," I answer lightly.

" But you feel no chill now ? " asks Tenicke, looking toward me.

I know my eyes are shining, my cheeks aglow.

" The sun was so warm," I answer irrelevantly.

For a second Tenicke regards me steadily, fixedly. Then I escape from all their glances as I turn and labor up the waste of sand in my water-logged garments. When I emerge from the bath-house, no longer a dripping mermaid, but clothed on with the nineteenth century righteousness of fine raiment, I perceive that there has been a change in the arrangement of the morning. Tenicke is waiting to take his place beside me on the back seat, while Colonel Chadwick drives with Letty on the front. For a moment I am glad with the gladness that came upon me a half hour ago ; but what is it — is it my own sneering, bitter spirit returned upon me, or is it Letty's *minauderies* — that changes the whole atmosphere, and makes everything seem so cheap and mean and trivial as we turn down the blossomy road that long ago I named my English lane ?

Tenicke, who is beside me, is no longer Jack's friend. He is the idle, *blasé* man, with an affected languor in his voice and manner, and a superciliousness and condescension which I hate. And as Letty tosses him her arch glances, and pouts her lips for his benefit, he pays her back with a detestable interest of lazy smiles and glances which fill me with a kind of shamed wonder. Is this the man, I say

to myself, at whose touch a half hour ago I flamed
and thrilled? As this thought, this question, assails
me I flame anew with a scorching misery of mortification. Then, all at once, again flash up my
mother's words: " If he likes one of my daughters "— And he likes my sister Letitia. This is
what these glances and smiles signify : in love with
my sister Letitia. I look at her fair, smooth, com-
placent face, that no love will ever line with an
anxious wrinkle, that no care will ever trace its
worry upon, and I remember the stinging emphasis
of judgment which Jack — my Jack — passed upon
her last year. He was watching her at her fooleries
with two or three young men at a party somewhere.
" I shall despise the man who falls in love with
Letty," he suddenly exclaimed to me ; and when
I said, " But girls must be girls, Jack, and you told
me the other night that *I* liked to flirt altogether
too well, sir," he returned, " And so you do, Rachel.
You 're a vain little coquette ; but you 're not of
Letty's kind. Letty 's so bloodless ; she does n't
feel; she has only sensations, and the greatest of
these is vanity."

As I look at her practicing her fooleries upon
Tenicke, as I turn and look at Tenicke himself, a
sense of loss comes over me. Must I despise Jack's
friend? And Jack? If he were here now and saw
his friend and his sister Letitia, would he keep his

word? would he be able to despise this man,
whom he had loved with a love passing the love
of woman?

That night there was a small party at dinner —
twelve in all; and as I sat at the end of the table
with Colonel Chadwick, and looked across at Tenicke, I thought I had never seen him in such a
brilliant, careless mood.   His dark eyes were
shining, his languid manner quite gone and in its
place a gayety that was almost boyish.   And once
or twice I met his eyes between the grapes and the
tall *épergne* of flowers, and was held in spite of myself by the bright and winsome look.

"How handsome Tenicke is," says Colonel Chadwick, as we dawdle over the dessert.   I do not answer this, and the Colonel does n't seem to expect
an answer; and he is only following out the train
of his own thoughts as he goes on, "And such a
lucky fellow as he's always been — born with a
gold spoon, you know.   I wonder" —

I lift my eyes at the sudden pause, and then I
follow the Colonel's glance, and see Barnet, the
waiter, crossing the room with a yellow envelope in
his hand — a telegram, and for Tenicke.   He breaks
off in the sentence he is in the middle of, and, with
the momentary surprise and expectancy one always
feels at a message upon his face, tears open the
wrapper.   "He has lost money upon one of those

horses," I instantly think, as I catch the sudden contraction of his brows and the compression of his lips.
But it must be a long message, I think, also, as the
seconds fly by, and he keeps that fixed look. I do
not know whether any one else marks all this, nor
whether the time seems so long to any one else before he lifts his head and resumes his place again,
and attempts to resume the old look — *attempts.* I
know very well it is only an attempt. Does anyone else know it? The light stream of talk flows
on, we all laugh and banter as we did five minutes
ago; but the real gayety has gone utterly out of
Tenicke's face, and I notice that he is doing what
is unusual with him, drinking very freely of champagne. "He must have lost heavily. What a
shame for men to do such things," I sum up with
irrelevant indignation. My indignation deepens as
I see the red flush rise to his cheek and the feverish
glitter in his eyes, and as I see, too, that his mother
is watching him anxiously. At the first possible
moment she rises from the table, and as we go
trooping into the parlor I find myself beside my
host, and we two the last of the company, and thus
in a measure alone together.

"Rachel!"

I look up at him in amazement. He has never
addressed me in this unceremonious manner, but
he does not heed my look. "Rachel," he repeats,

"what was the name of Jack's friend in Colorado
— that banking friend of his?"

"I — I don't know," I stammer in answer.

"Does your mother know? could she find out?"

"She might."

Some one speaks to him here, and he moves away. Presently I see him standing under the chandelier, laughing and talking much as usual; but I fall to wondering, as I note the deepening flush upon his cheek, if his talk is as odd and inconsequent as his words to me; and as I regard him a swift, subtle, external change seems to have come over him. He looks all at once dissolute and degenerate. While he stands there Barnet comes in with the mail. There are several letters and the New York papers. Colonel Chadwick, as is his custom, possesses himself of the paper, and runs his swift glance over the telegraphic column without breaking his frothy talk with pretty Mrs. Maverick. But in a moment he turns, forgetting all his fine manners, and reads aloud, in an excited tone, that first announcement of the Jay Cooke failure which so startled the whole world at the time.

There is a various outcry from various voices, notes of speculation, wonder, and dismay. Most of the auditors feel the shock evidently, yet as evidently it is a recoverable shock. But Tenicke Ditworth! For a few minutes, I had lost sight of him. Now I turn to look at him. In that look I see all at once how I have blundered for the last twenty minutes. There is no perceptible change in his face. IIe sits idly drumming upon the table near him, but I am perfectly certain that this intelligence is not so new to him as to us; that not half an hour since he had read the announcement privately conveyed in that telegram over which he had lingered so long. And he had read with it his own ruin. I wondered then, I wonder now, that no one seemed to see what I did. Perhaps, however, they were wiser than I thought, and kept their own well-bred, unasking counsel.

At any rate the party breaks up much earlier than parties usually break up at the Ditworths'. When the door closes upon the last guest Tenicke returns to the little waiting group in the parlor, and, with no sign now of excitement, says coolly, —

"I must catch the early train to-morrow morning *en route* for New York. This affair is going to tell hardly upon us."

He seems to address himself to Colonel Chadwick, and the colonel answers, —

"Yes; I thought so by your silence. I had no idea before that you were involved there, or I should n't have read" —

"Oh, that did n't matter. I had the news by telegram already."

My mother here rises, and we girls follow her example, and as we say good-night I know very well that it is good-by; but I little think what a long time it will be before I see Jack's friend again.

II.

"Letty may go to the Cargills', mother, and I will stay with you. I shall like that much better."

"But you need a change, Rachel; you are not very strong this summer."

"I should n't get stronger at the Cargills'. I never cared for the Cargill girls; they tire me. But Letty gets on with them admirably."

My mother sighs and says no more. She is glad to have me with her, I know, but she is so truly unselfish that she will urge my leaving her if she thinks it is for my good. By and by Letty comes in, flushed and a little cross, her hands full of parcels. I acquaint her with my determination to stay at home instead of accepting the Cargills' invitation.

"Well, you can do as you like, of course, Ray, but I should think you 'd want to go *somewhere*, and the Cargills' seems our only chance *this* summer. If it had n't been for that horrid, hateful failure last year, we might be at the Ditworths' this minute."

"And we might *not*," I answer rather snappishly.

Letty flings up her head. " *You* might not. I am quite sure *I* should have been there, and very likely I might have invited you to pass the summer with me, Miss Rachel."

"Don't be silly, Letty, or at least any sillier than you can help. If Tenicke Ditworth had had such an interest in you as you imply, he would n't have let you remain in such ignorance of him all these months," I break out hotly.

" 'Tenicke Ditworth is a man of sense and some honor, I suppose, and of course he is very well aware that it would be in the very highest degree dishonorable for a man who is entirely without means to ask a girl to become his wife."

I hold my peace now. I always get the worst of it with Letty; she is so self-complacent, so entirely convinced of her own power, of her own judgment. I hold my peace, but inwardly I am in anything but a peaceful frame of mind. It is eight, ten months ago since I bade Tenicke Ditworth good-by, and no word from him has come to us since. I *know* now that Letty never had his heart. I knew it when he said good-by there; when he held her hand for the moment and *did not see her*. Equally as well I know too — I do not lie to myself any more — I know that Tenicke Dit-

worth is more, immeasurably more, to me, than
Jack's friend.   And *he?*   I look back to that last
day when he held me in his arms while the waves
dashed over us, when his kind voice questioned of
my safety, and later, in that last good-by, the
glance that held me for an instant as his arms held
me a few hours before.   This is all I have — very
insufficient food for love to feed on; but I have
grown quite shameless in these last ten months.   I
may be no more to him than Jack's sister, but I
love him, love him, love him!   He is to me the
one man in all the world; and if I think now and
again of the faults I found in him, I think with re-
morse and humiliation of the bitter spirit, the de-
mon of jealousy, which clouded my vision through
all that summer time.

And here with the summer again I am as utterly
separated from him as if he had gone into that un-
discovered country where I lost sight of my dear
Jack so little while, and yet so long ago.   But yet
I am certain he is not dead.   I am certain that
some day I shall see him again, as I saw him ten
months ago; some day I shall hear his voice and
feel the clasp of his hand.   But in the mean time,
during this waiting summer, I choose my own
thoughts for company, instead of Letty and the
Cargill girls.   And Letty is quite content with my
decision.   She is not so obtuse but that she feels

now and then my critical spirit. But one day, as
she sits plaiting a ruffle for her throat, — it is the
day before her departure, — she says to me quite
suddenly, as if the idea had all at once dawned
upon her, " I think it is very strange, Rachel, that
we have never heard from the Ditworths any way,
don't you ? "

" I don't know that I do. When Colonel Chadwick went to Europe, last autumn, we lost our only
link between us and the Ditworths."

" But I should have thought that Mrs. Ditworth
would have written to mother."

" Mrs. Ditworth ? Why should she ? After all,
our acquaintance was a very new one. We had
only met the summer before at Rye, and her interest was through her son Tenicke's interest " — I
have an inward tremor as I pronounce this name,
like Tennyson's " Fatima " — " was through Tenicke's interest in us for Jack's sake."

" And so you think it was for Jack's sake entirely that we were invited for that month at Newport ? "

I resume my book, disdaining to reply to this
vain question so vainly asked with all Letty's sim-
pering complacence. But presently I hear a new
tone in my sister's voice.

" Rachel, Rachel, come here ! "

She is sitting by the window, and I am lying

upon the lounge with a book in my hand. I look up incuriously, but still perceptive of her change of tone.

" Rachel, is n't this funny? Here is that Newport ice man, who looked so much like Tenicke."

I do not wait for another call; in a second I am on my feet and looking over Letty's shoulder at the stalwart figure just leaving the gate. Letty goes chattering on, but I cannot speak to her. My heart is beating up in my throat, and I am trembling and cold to my fingers' ends. The sight of that tall, sinewy figure, clad in a blue flannel shirt and black trousers, suddenly obliterates all these ten long months, and I am sitting on a wide piazza, listening to the " swiff, swiff" of the lawn mowers and an occasional news item read in a fluent voice at my elbow, or I am —

" He is n't so like as I thought," says Letty, presently. I look with a last scrutiny as the man mounts the wagon, and I am constrained to admit that Letty is right. I am looking at a man of more muscular build than Tenicke Ditworth, with a face of red bronze entirely wanting in that fine Vandyke outline and brown silk beard of which I used to think that Jack's friend was so vain. But in spite of these differences, all the rest of the day I feel as if I was haunted. I go about the house with Tenicke's low voice in my ears, and with a close

crowding memory of glance and touch and presence
that at last gives me the only dream of him in my
sleep that I have had since I parted from him.

The next day Letty goes, and I am alone with
my mother and our one small servant; for, as Letty has said, the great panic has not passed us by,
and we are by no means as comfortable in our circumstances as last year at this time. Letty goes,
and I am left to my dreams undisturbed; and they
don't "dim their fine gold" as the days go on.
Vivid and clear they crowd upon me, until I am
driven into a kind of desperation of desire that I
must make them reality. I think with a shudder
that it was just this wild trouble of fancied reality
that haunted me when Jack died. Was Tenicke
Ditworth dead? But I knew myself the most
unreasonable, the most besotted of mortal women
when I asked this question of myself; for I am
perfectly well aware that the daily contemplation
of what Letty was pleased to call Tenicke's double
is really at the bottom of all these vivid fancies —
the material upon which my hungry heart and impatient nature has been building up these airy
structures. Day after day I place myself at the
window and peer at the red bronze face which is
like, yet so unlike Tenicke Ditworth's. And every
day I am startled by the strange likeness in unlikeness. Every day my pulses get some new impetus

from some new suggestion, some trick of movement
or glance. My mother sits reading a letter from
Letty one morning. "What is this," she suddenly
asks, "about Mr. Ditworth? 'Does Tenicke's
Double still bring you ice?'"

I hasten to explain Letty's fancied resemblance.
I say nothing of my own fancy about it. And
presently, as the gate clangs, my mother goes to
the window to satisfy herself of this resemblance.
After a moment's observation she turns away in-
differently with but one remark : —

" Letty has very odd ideas of likeness."

" And you don't think there is any likeness?" I
ask amazed.

" To Mr. Ditworth? Not the slightest ; not
more than there would be between any two men
of rather exceptionally fine physique and of that
dark type. This man is larger, but not so tall as
Mr. Ditworth, and with a heavier and coarser
build."

Is all this resemblance after all half imagination?
As I ask myself this question I watch this man of
coarser and heavier build mount to the wagon seat
and drive off down the street. At that moment
certainly I could see with my mother's eyes, and I
could find no likeness to Tenicke Ditworth.

It is at the latter part of this very day that my
mother, regarding me earnestly and a little anxiously
a moment, says : —

" Rachel, you are growing thin with this confinement to the city. I think I did wrong in not insisting upon your going with Letty."

" Mother, I could *not* stand the Cargill girls and Letty in a lump. *That* would make a skeleton of me in a week," I answer with vehement emphasis.

" What unreasoning prejudices you do have, Rachel."

" I suppose all prejudices are unreasoning. It is n't a matter of reason, but of instinct and unlikeness. We are not of the same kind. Mother " — I am sore and irritable, or I should never have said· this — " Jack felt *just* as I did about Letty, always."

A flush crosses my mother's face. She remembers all Jack's little trials with pretty, foolish Letty, remembers them with pain, as mothers must the natural antagonisms of their children. But she says no more of my going to the Cargills', and I think she has forgotten my thin face until she hands me an invitation to spend a week with an old friend of hers two or three miles from the city. I did not care specially to go, but when I find myself in the sweet country air once more, and scent the mown fields, and see the " far blue hills," I begin to relent of my apathy and feel that it is good to be alive and young. And when I find on the second day that there is to be " a garden party " in the great old-fashioned pretty garden which seems to lie all about the house, I am more interested in my fineries than I have been for months; and when I find at this party a rather handsome young man, who is of much consequence apparently to all the young women present, but who turns from their charms and persists in becoming my attendant cavalier, I am very far from displeased thereat, and am quite easily persuaded to drop "that everlasting croquet mallet" and go on a tour of investigation down the queer, quaint ways of the winding footpaths. That night when I stand crimping my hair before the mirror I look at my brightened face, and recall Jack's judgment of me — "a vain little flirt." As the days go by I see no reason to doubt this judgment; for my fine garden cavalier, who turns out to be a near neighbor, makes himself my sole protector in sundry explorations over "the far blue hills."

At the end of the week my mother comes for me, as she had planned.

"Ah, I knew you needed a change, Rachel," she says, in a pleased voice. "You are looking quite like yourself again."

"*Is n't* she ?" repeats my hostess.

Then presently I see the two walking in the old garden and talking earnestly together. When a little later my new acquaintance, Mr. Richard Parsons, saunters up the steps, I see my hostess telegraph by a glance to my mother, and I guess at once all the mystery of that conference.

Mr. Parsons is one of the young men of whom mothers are sure to approve. He is well-looking and well-behaved, a genial, kindly soul, upon whom the world has showered good fortune befitting the good qualities. He is, to sum it all up, a safe man, and it is upon this safe man that I am expected to bestow myself. That this is the subject matter of the conference between my mother and her friend I do not need to be told.

Until now I had never thought seriously of Mr. Parsons's possible feeling; I had been a vain little flirt, but an unthinking one. But now I recall his looks, his tones, and a something *empressé* in his manner, which I had taken carelessly enough before, but which return upon me with a fuller meaning. It had been a long summer day to *me* — a day of transient pleasure, wherein I had rested a moment *while I waited.* To Richard Parsons it had been but the *beginning* of a summer which stretched out into an illimitable future. If I guessed at all this in that moment of retrospection, I have amplest confirmation in another week, for in that time Mr. Parsons has come to the point, and plainly declared his intentions, undeterred by the sudden stiffness which my awakened conscience has infused at that late day into my manner. His evident astonishment at my rejection of his suit is sufficiently humiliating, without the curious amazement of my mother's friend, and the surprised disappointment of my mother herself.

" You seemed to like him so much, Rachel."

" I *did like* him, but that is a very different matter from loving."

" It is often much safer to begin life with another on the *liking* you speak of than what young people call love," answered my mother with singular asperity.

I am dumb after this argument. Do all people, I wonder, outlive this love which is the burden of every poet's song since the world began? I remember an old story I have heard about my mother's beauty in her youth and the lovers that she had. " Your mother had the finest opportunities of any of us, and she married the poorest of them all," my aunt Catherine had often said to me, with a sharp frankness exceedingly unflattering to my father. I gather from this that it was most decidedly a love match, and I look at the handsome face of my paternal parent as it appears in the crayon portrait above my head, and hunt up all my childish memories to recall his pleasant voice and winning ways. I suppose that he once delighted my mother with this pleasant voice, and with these winning ways ; I suppose that she once thrilled at the touch of his hand or the sound of his footsteps like any love-smitten girl. But now, this "light that was never on sea or land," has faded into worse than nothingness.

I think of a voice whose every intonation I know so well, of eyes that I could never meet even in my time of bitter cavil and jealousy without a quickened pulsation. Will there come a day when I shall look back with indifference, when I shall be able to meet the eyes and hear the voice perhaps with dulled senses? Now, with my blood at fever heat, I answer vehemently, No, no, no! But how can I promise for myself? How can I say that I shall make exception to the myriads who, like my mother, "preach down a daughter's heart," having overlived the purple light of love and youth? But I have nothing to do with that gray and empty future day. I *will* have nothing to do with it. Here is my youth, and with it my love that may never come nearer to me than now. But even so, I know, I know, that "all other pleasures are not worth its pains." As I come to this triumphant conclusion, as I feel that nothing, nothing can ever dim *my* "light that was never on sea or land," I get a letter from my sister with this piece of information : —

"What do you think? Tom Cargill has come home from Colorado, and he says that his cousin

Harry, saw Tenicke Ditworth about twenty miles from Denver, and that he has married a rich widow, and is coming East shortly to buy back the Newport estate."

All in a moment, "down go tower and temple." Shame and humiliation assail me. I have been living in an ideal world, and bowing down, like many another foolish woman, before an ideal hero. Poor and unfortunate, struggling with adverse fate, I had seen my hero, and in that condition had glorified him, had felt that I had a right in him. But what had I to do with a man who had smartly retrieved his fortunes by marrying a rich widow?

"What does Letty say?" asks my mother, coming into the room when I had arrived at this point. I hand the letter to her. She skims it through, but makes no comment. But as she returns it to me I ask suddenly, —

"Mother, did Mr. Ditworth ask you about Jack's friend in Colorado before he went away?"

"Yes, he asked me after dinner that day the news arrived in Newport of the Jay Cooke failure. It was Jacob Vanstart, you know. I gave him his name. That was sufficient, for Mr. Vanstart was the richest man in Colorado. I presume Mr. Ditworth wanted his influence in entering into some business; and I should n't be surprised if he had married Mr. Vanstart's widowed sister, Mrs. Baum."

So this was the end of my dreams! Married to Mrs. Baum!

"Mother, do you suppose Tenicke Ditworth had this — this Mrs. Baum in his mind — I mean was that his business, to go out there and look up Mr. Vanstart's rich widowed sister?" I am reckless just now how I trample on and 'deface the clay image I have been worshiping.

"What a foolish question, Rachel," my mother replies to this. "It is n't at all likely that Mr. Ditworth knew anything of Mr. Vanstart's sister; or, if he did, that he would project such an undertaking in a moment."

I laugh feebly, and then all at once the room becomes intolerable to me. Everything seems dwarfed and pinched, narrow and mean. I go out upon the little side stoop for a breath of fresh air. As I stand there pulling down some half-starved honeysuckle blossoms, the gate creaks on its rusty hinge, and I look up to see *Tenicke Ditworth's Double!*

The honeysuckle springs back from my hand, and my heart beats up in my throat again, as the strange resemblance strikes me anew. How like, oh, how like he is! For an instant, just an instant, I forget Letty's news, forget everything but the face that is recalled to me. Then, swift and sharp, everything returns upon me, and I am try-

ing to reconcile this face, the sweet, kind eyes Jack
used to talk about, with Mrs. Baum's husband.

Well, the days go by; time gets on in a slow,
sluggish fashion with me; I eat and drink, laugh
and talk with my mother and the few guests we
have, much as usual; but something has gone out
of the days, and life seems disjointed and savorless.
When I sit down to think now, there is no region
of memory where I can rest apart from Jack and
Jack's friend. Ever since I have had a young girl's
thoughts, they have been interwoven with Jack and
this friend of his. And now — well, I try hard,
all through the dull afternoons and the duller even-
ings, to interest myself in the neighborly talk that
comes in my way. But in the mornings, with a
fool's insensate folly — in the mornings I render my
afternoon and evening task as difficult as possible
by the observation I take at the side window of a
certain stalwart figure whose every motion recalls
with painful distinctness the man I am trying to
put out of my mind and heart!' In this consistent
occupation all the little summer bloom I had gained
fades, and my thin cheeks grow thinner yet, until
there are ugly hollows under the cheek-bones, and
small wrinkled ripples beneath my eyes. But
when did happy or unhappy lovers ever conduct
themselves consistently? Do I call myself a lover
still, with my hero a hero no longer? I do not call

myself anything. I only feel that the past and I cannot separate without long throes of pain which I cannot measure. I only know that when I try to wrench myself away from my memories I am, like Milne's lover, in worse than an empty world.

So the dreary, dusty days go on from bad to worse. When I look at myself in the glass now, I see a face unknown before; pale, and growing every morning paler still, and at night a hot red color burning in two hard outlined spots upon my cheeks. I have read all my life sentimental stories of young women pining away for love, and I suppose I thought it was a very pretty thing to do. But if this is what I am doing, it is anything but a pretty piece of business. I am not dying, nor on the road to it. I am simply growing unhealthy and ugly as fast as possible. Womanlike, a feeling of resentment kindles within me at this contingency. To lose love and happiness and one's good looks all together is a threefold tragedy. So with jeering bitterness I appeal to myself against myself, as I sit late on Saturday afternoon beneath the dried-up honeysuckle on the little side porch, where, when the wind comes from the south, a small puff will now and then find its way over our high board fence. Everybody has gone away for the evening, and I am left alone to keep house and nurse my foolish fancies. " Creak, creak," the cart wheels lazily roll over the pavement outside, and now and then the swift, smart rattle of a smart carriage, and two or three organ-grinders belaboring their wheezy old instruments, in the vain attempt to produce melody.　I am listening to all this with a dull ear and humming mechanically the "Blue Danube" waltz in broken time with the nearest organ, when the gate swings open.

"No, no," I call out.　"Don't come any nearer." Then I stop in dismay.　It is not the grimacing young scamp of an organ-grinder I expected, but a tall, well-known figure in a navy-blue shirt.　I forget to explain my words in my surprise at this appearance at this hour.　But as the tall figure sways past me, heavily laden with an extra amount of ice, I remember that it is Saturday night; that the day has been unusually warm, and so the belated time. I feel a little quiver of excitement as I make up my mind in the next moment to speak with this curious Double as he comes back.　For I must explain my sharp exclamation; one must be decent even to an ice man.　Presently I hear his step crunching the gravel, and I meet him face to face as he turns the corner of the lattice.　"I thought it was an organ-grinder when I spoke as you opened the gate," I began.　Then I look up, standing quite near as I am, and I see, in the deep amber sunset light — I see a smile slowly, then swiftly, breaking out of

eyes and lips, a smile that can only, only belong —
"Oh, Tenicke! Tenicke!" In a moment more I
wonder for just a dizzy second or two if I am gone
clean mad, for I am clinging fast to the blue-shirted
arm and laughing and crying in a breath, "Oh,
Tenicke! Tenicke!" Just a dizzy second or two,
then I drag him in through the doorway, through
the little side hall, into the cool empty parlor. The
sunset light streams in through the half-open shut-
ter, and falls in one clear strong ray across the face,
not of any stranger, of any vexatious Double, but
the face — yes, the face of Tenicke Ditworth himself.

"To think you did n't know me before, Rachel.
I should make my fortune as an actor, should n't
I?" He smiles down at me, but there are tears in
his eyes, in his voice; and at the sight, at the sound,
I forget all about that foolish story of Mrs. Baum,
all my proper decencies and proprieties are scattered to the winds, and I cast myself upon Tenicke
Ditworth's breast, and out of my suddenly relieved
heart, heedless of everything but the present, I
make love, fond, desperate, shameless love, to our
ice man.

By and by I lift my head. The sunset glory has
gone, but the new-risen moon shines full in my
darling's face — *my* darling's, not Mrs. Baum's, nor
poor, pretty, shallow Letty's, as I had foolishly

fancied once, but mine, mine always from the very first, as I knew now; and it is now for the first time I ask a question, a question that the one great fact of presence had put aside for these swift minutes.

"How did it all happen? How did it come to this?"

"How did it come to *this*?" and he touched his blue shirt with a half laugh. "Rachel, I don't suppose you can have any idea how quickly a fortune can take wings. I don't think *I* had until I found at the end of a few months that I could n't raise a dollar without borrowing. I tried in the mean time to find some occupation, but my idle, desultory life had unfortunately left me at very loose ends in business adaptability; and besides that, it was a terrible time; all the situations were filled, and thousands like myself were out of employment. I was walking down Broadway one morning considering what I should try next, when I met Jim Borland, whose father is the largest ice dealer you have in your city. In an instant I recalled our banter at Newport, and thought to myself that as I could n't find an occupation to suit *me*, I might as well suit the occupation to myself. When I sounded Jim, he supposed I was after a clerkship in the counting-room. Good fellow, he would have turned somebody out for me if he could, but that was out of the question. When I told him it was a carrier's place I proposed to take, you ought to have seen his face. I believe for a moment he thought I had been drinking, or that my losses had turned my brain. When he found that I was in earnest, he tried to dissuade me from my notion, as he called it. Something would be sure to turn up in a month or two, and in the mean time he would be my banker. But I was already in debt, and I knew better than he how unlikely anything of the kind that he supposed fitted for me was likely to turn up for the waiting. Well, that night I left New York with him, and two days after I was installed in my carrier's route."

" But *how* came you" —

" To be at *your* part of the city, and at your door? I had your address, Rachel, and I was such a romantic fool that I wanted to get a glimpse of you now and then; and a little spirit of fun possessed me too, the whole thing was so absurd. I had really no idea of wooing you, my dear girl, in this melodramatic sort of disguise. I was n't proposing to play theatre. But I wanted to see if you 'd know me, and it took you all summer " —

" If it had n't been for that curious Double of yours, that man who was so like you last season, I should never have doubted for an instant. But Tenicke, what does your mother think of all this? '

"She does n't know it.   She had a few thousands secured, thank God, elsewhere; and her health failing in all the worry and excitement, I got her off to Geneva with Chadwick and his sister.   So you see I am working out the problem alone, Rachel.   And I don't have altogether a bad time of it.   I get six hundred dollars a year, and it suffices me, for I don't live the life of a dandy now.   I have one room six miles out of town where I sleep, and where on Sundays I cook my own dinner and read Thoreau and Emerson."   He laughs a little, holding me away with two strong arms that he may look in my face.   After a moment he resumes: " Rachel, there 's to be a vacancy in the counting-room next month, and the general, old Mr. Borland, has offered it to me.   And, Rachel, this is not all.   I have found that out of the wreck of half a million I shall finally rescue five or six thousand dollars, and I 'm going to put it into this ice business.   Rachel, will you marry me on these prospects ? "

" I 'll marry you now, Tenicke, on the six hundred dollars."

" To-morrow, then ; that 's the carriers' holiday. My wedding suit will be out of fashion — a year old, Rachel ; and you 'll have to keep house with me in my one room and make my coffee at five o'clock in the morning."

"I can make better coffee than you ever tasted, sir."

We look at each other a moment, laughing, both of us; then suddenly the arms that have been holding me off for a better look at my foolishly fond face draw me nearer, and I am winking and blinking against our ice man's blue flannel shirt collar.

Two months from that time we are married. I do not go to housekeeping in one room, certainly, but in a ridiculously small cottage ten miles out of town. Letty, looking on, does not envy me, but she only says, "To think that Tenicke Ditworth should turn out nothing but an ice man after all."

IN THE RED ROOM.

 SHALL have to put you in the red room, Jenny. I had kept the east chamber for you, but we do have so much unexpected company anniversary week. Last night Mrs. Deane came with her baby, and the red room is so far away that I did n't feel as if it was just the thing to put her there."

"No, of course not, and I 'm sure I 'd as lief sleep in the red room as the east room."

"Mary Ann will sleep on the lounge in the room, so you won't mind."

"For mercy's sake, Martha, what *do* you think I want Mary Ann to sleep in the room with me for?"

"I was afraid you might get nervous, so far off from the rest of the rooms."

"Get nervous! why I should never think of such a thing. What should I get nervous about? You have n't a burglar epidemic just now, have you, or perhaps a walking ghost?"

"N-o, not exactly."

At this reply Jenny Merryweather turned suddenly from the contemplation of her new traveling suit which the pier-glass before her reflected in all its beauties, turned suddenly and confronted her friend with her inquiring look.

" Martha Carrique, it *is* a ghost, and you were going to smuggle me into his den actually without proper warning or introduction."

" You ridiculous girl, there 's no ghost about it, but there *is* a foolish story connected with the room I thought you had heard."

" Only a story of a ghost ! Only the ghost of a ghost ! Oh dear, Martha, what a disappointment. I did hope it was one of the veritable old colonial gentry such as used to be here once in the flesh and blood. Perhaps Colonel Carrique himself, or one of the Hancock family, or that beautiful great, great, great aunt or grandmother of yours, whom Governor Hancock had to send home, because the Indian chief fell in love with her. But on the whole, I 'd rather it was that handsome Colonel Carrique in his royalist red coat, though it might n't be so proper, for I *am* so tired of seeing nothing but women, Martha, that I prefer even a visiting ghost to be a masculine one."

" You ridiculous girl ! " repeated Mrs. Carrique, going off into one of her little spasms of laughter.

" That 's the second time you 've called me that,

Martha.   But just think what an out-and-out lark
this is for me.   Six months tied down to that b-a
ba, b-i bi, b-o bo, business, in that dear, dull,
deserted-of-mankind, little native town of mine.
Positively, Martha, there is n't but one young man
left in the place, and he 's rather *non compos.*   And
for the rest, for the older ones, the married men,
you never saw such ungallant creatures.   No woman need be jealous of her husband in our town,
Martha.   If Frank gets frisky here, you just bring
him down to Balem, there 's something in the very
air there that takes all the frisk out of them.   Why,
I went to a school-meeting one night, Martha, where
I happened to be the only lady with seven gentlemen.   Well, my dear, what do you think — those
seven men allowed me to walk home — a quarter of
a mile — alone.   Not one of them had the polite-
ness, the decency, to offer himself as an escort.
Stop, Martha, you need n't call me a ridiculous
girl again; I 'm not embroidering in the least, I 'm
telling you a downright fact.   The worst of it was,
the injurious effect upon my self-esteem.   I was n't
at all afraid to walk through our Puritanic little
streets even if it had been midnight, but to have
seven men unite in showing you that you were not
sufficiently agreeable to charm them out of their
stolid, selfish laziness even into momentary good
manners *was* humiliating.   Suppose they *had* known

me all their lives ? What had that to do with it ? Oh, I tell you, Martha, I have n't held up my head since ! " and Jenny Merryweather disclosed all her little milk-white teeth at this announcement. Sauntering along the wide halls, and the queer passageways in this queer old house, the two girls — for Mrs. Carrique, spite of her matronly honors, was only one of the Saturday Reviewers " great girls " —came just at this crisis of the conversation to the red room in question. This room was situated in the northwest corner of the house, in what was called " the gable end." It was divided from the other bed-chambers by a long passage opening from the main hall by a narrow door. Seen in the noon sunshine, it looked the cosiest chamber in the world, with its red carpet and curtains, and the pretty outlook upon the gardens and the green hills of Middlesex County. But that night when Mrs. Carrique accompanied her young guest again through the halls and passage-ways, and finally entered the isolated room to see if her not peculiarly reliable chambermaid had discharged her duty thoroughly, the red room had lost its cheerful aspect, and by the light of the two candles the red carpet and draperies took on a sombre depth and shade that was by no means enlivening, or at least such was the opinion of the hostess herself on this second visit. Jenny was chattering away as usual, and seemed to be entirely unobservant of the change which night had wrought in her surroundings.

"It does look *so* lonesome here at night," at last broke out Mrs. Carrique, "that I do think you had better have Mary Ann sleep on the lounge."

Jenny stopped pulling out the twenty-six hair-pins that held that marvelous structure of braids and curls and frizzes together, and turning round from the mirror looked with real and not affected astonishment at her friend.

"Martha, *I* think you are getting hipped in this old trap. The idea of your talking to me about nerves. Have n't we a whole pack of ghosts in Balem, and one a regular old witch? Nervous! my dear, feel of that arm," and with a gay little smile she held out a round, white member, the healthy firmness of which told an enviable story of circulation and digestion. "That means pulling oars with Jimmy and beating him at that," this merry little Jenny went on, nodding and smiling; "and it means, too, Mrs. Martha Carrique, that I am so sound and healthy, as Aunt Desire says, 'so rudely healthy,' that if I 'have any nerves they are completely out of sight and out of mind. So now you can just go to bed and to sleep without any more worry about me, or threats of Mary Ann."

Mrs. Carrique, thus adjured, takes a final survey of window and door fastenings, and bids her guest good-night.   And not many minutes after Jenny Merryweather, having disposed of those twenty-six hair-pins and the structure of braids and curls and frizzes, is snugly ensconced between the clover-scented sheets, sleeping the sleep of the just.

" And to think, Frank, that I forgot to tell her the ghost story after all," says Mrs. Martha, as she rejoins her husband.

" All the better that you did n't repeat that foolish stuff."

" Well, I don't think that anything would disturb Jenny. I never saw such a girl. It was n't so strange that *I* should forget that I had n't told her the story, but that she should care so little as to ask no questions on what is usually so interesting to girls."

" But Jenny has been brought up on ghost stories. Balem is full of 'em, you know. She came here for something new, Martha."

At the breakfast table the next morning Jenny appeared with the brightest of faces.

" Well," she said laughingly, " your ghost did n't pay me a visit, Martha, but I *did* have the queerest dream."

" I hope it was a pleasant one; you know what the sign is about the first dream under a strange roof."

" That it will come true ; well, I don't think my dream is likely to come true," and Jenny laughed again.

"You 've no objection to telling it to us,. have you?" asked Mr. Carrique.

"Oh, not in the least. I went to sleep almost as quick as my head touched the pillow, and it was in this first sleep that I met your ancestor Colonel Carrique. You know we had been speaking of him, Martha, and I had admired his portrait and told you that if I was to be visited by a ghost I should prefer the handsome royalist. Well I dreamed that I was at a great party in this very house, only the furniture was all of it quite old-fashioned, and instead of your big windows there were ever so many smaller ones, and so high from the floor they looked like prison windows to me"—

"Well, I declare, Jenny that was the very appearance the house presented before we altered it. Did I ever give you that description of it?"

"No, I am sure you did n't, for the only letter I got from you after you purchased the house was an invitation to visit you, and as I have n't seen you since, until yesterday, and Frank answered my note to you by a telegram that he would meet me at 2 P. M., Wednesday, I don't see where you could have told your story of improvements."

"Oh, I dare say she told you yesterday, Miss Jenny, when you first arrived."

"Indeed she did n't, Mr. Carrique. I don't lose my memory quite so easily as that," answered Jenny, laughing, but a little nettled.

"I see, I see, you are bound to put it all to the red room account," Mr. Carrique returned, gayly.

Jenny looked at him with a rather puzzled face, but Mrs. Carrique sent her off of that track, by saying, "Come, do go on with your dream, Jenny. There's nothing I like so much to hear about as people's dreams."

Thus adjured, Jenny went on. "When I came into the room where all these gentry were, the first person I saw distinctly was a tall, handsome man, in a red royalist uniform just like that in the picture of Colonel Carrique, and the face of this gentleman was precisely like the face in the portrait. He came forward to meet me as I entered, and as he stood before me a moment what *do* you think he said?" And here pausing, Jenny laughs and actually blushes a little.

"We give it up; none of this family are good at conundrums, Jenny," Frank Carrique remarks; and so with another little laugh, and another little blush Jenny proceeds again:—

"He said in such a low tone that I understood at once that nobody but myself was expected to hear it: 'Miss Merryweather, my nephew has arrived, and is impatient to meet his promised wife.' The next moment he turned about and a young man not at all like the colonel and dressed in the fashion of to-day stood before me. He put out his

hand to take mine, and as he did so I started back
in a sort of fright, whereupon the old colonel bent
down and whispered in my ear, ‘It is of no use for
you to resist, my dear; it is your fate.’

“ This only frightened me the more, and I turned
and ran out of the room as fast as my feet could
carry me. The colonel ran after me not at all in a
rage but laughing immoderately. But I was too
swift for him. I ran straight to the red room and
banged the door in his face. At that instant I
awoke, laughing myself. I lay awake a few moments, and then falling fast asleep again, I took up
my dream just where I left off, for I heard the
sound of the colonel’s laughter growing fainter and
fainter, and the sound of his footsteps as he went
down the stairs. I had escaped the colonel, but
there before me stood an old, old lady with a
white satin dress over her arm. ‘It’s of no use
for you to resist,’ she said, repeating the colonel’s
words and wagging her head wickedly at me, ‘it’s
your fate;’ and then wagging her head still more,
‘ for this prank of yours, you will be married to-
night, Miss.’ Do what I would I could n’t seem to
escape from the old woman, until after that white
satin dress had been donned, and then as she opened
the door and seized my wrist to lead me down, I
sprung away, but my foot caught in my grand gown,
and I felt myself falling in that horrid way one

does in dreams. While I was falling, I awoke again. I lay awhile speculating about my odd dream, and the special oddity of my resuming it in the manner I had. And in this speculation I fell asleep once more, and once more *resumed the same thread.* This time I was lying in a great canopied bed in that very red room, and the old lady and the colonel were standing before me looking as solemn as judges. The old lady came close up to the bed, and leaning over me, said in a shrill little voice: 'You won't escape us again, Miss, I can tell you. That ancestress of yours served this family a nice trick in her day, and got us well scandalized by her folly.' Then that handsome colonel laughed, and said in the politest way: 'And you, my dear, are going to atone for all that. You 'll unite' — and snap here went the thread again. I suppose it was that horrid little black-and-tan terrier of yours who was yapping under my window that woke me this time. I went to sleep again, but I did n't resume my dream again, and I did so want to hear what the colonel was going to say."

"The fact of it is, you were disappointed in not meeting that nephew again, Miss Jenny," said Frank Carrique, jocosely.

"But was n't it a very odd dream, taking the fact of my resuming it twice after waking?" asked Jenny here, giving no heed to Mr. Carrique's facetia.

" Well, yes, it was rather odd, but still that fact
of resuming a dream is n't uncommon."

" No, I don't know that it is," returns Jenny,
feeling somehow by Mr. Carrique's words and manner as if she had been telling a very foolish and
uninteresting story. Martha, too, looked dull and
distraite, and that little Mrs. Deane had a queer,
constrained expression as if she were laughing at
her. Abashed at first by these indications, our
little school-mistress at the second turn of her
thought became considerably nettled; and being a
rather quick-tempered little lady, there is no knowing what sarcastic expression she might have found,
if just at the moment a diversion had not been
created by the arrival of fresh guests. Before the
day was over the fresh guests and the fresh scenes,
and Martha's real pleasure in her society shown
at every turn, dispelled the little cloud entirely.
Later, the memory, not the cloud itself, came before her with a new significance. But this was so
late, at the very end of her visit, indeed, that we
won't talk of it just now. In the interim lay all
that beautiful time of summer, and freedom from
what she called that b-a ba, b-i bi, b-o bo business;
the weary little round of her primary school duties.

There has come to be a saying in Boston that
has almost passed into a proverb, that it always
rains anniversary week; but on this anniversary·

of Jenny's first visit to her friend since that friend had arrived at the dignity of matronhood, and an ancestral mansion, on this first and most eventful visit of hers, the May sky refused to weep its usual anniversary tears, and the sun shone, with the thermometer in the eighties for days. But in and out, in and out, sometimes by horse-car and sometimes in Mr. Carrique's pretty beach wagon, our little Yankee school-mistress took her way in the dust and heat to listen to the heresies in Tremont Temple, or the more orthodox controversies in Music Hall.

"How you *can* stand so much theology and philosophy, I don't see, Jenny," exclaimed Mrs. Martha, one morning towards the end of the week, as Jenny came down equipped for her daily excursion. "And what's more, Jenny, how you can comprehend it all passes me."

"Comprehend it? bless me," ejaculated Jenny briskly; "I don't pretend to comprehend half of it. Why, Martha, I go to see the people; to meet my friends and acquaintances. You don't consider that I 'm a country girl compared to you, and that I 'm on a vacation lark, and mean to make the most of my time."

"Goodness gracious!" cried Mrs. Martha, at this, ",and I thought, and Frank thought, all the time, that you were up to all those isms; and you just go there for nothing in the world but to meet the people, like any other girl."

"Yes, did you expect I was n't like any other girl, I should like to know, Martha Carrique?"

"Why, yes, in a way I suppose I did.　And you are, you know, Jenny, rather on the intellectual pattern compared to me."

Jenny laughed. "Compared to you!　My superior intellect, I suppose, is shown in teaching an infant-school, and not being afraid of ghosts.　That last virtue, however, is only a matter of physical health.　But, by the way, Martha, you have n't told me your ghost story yet, and now 's your time. I 've got just twenty minutes before the car starts."

Martha "looks queer."　"Oh, it 's nothing but an old tale about the colonel and some friend of his appearing now and then."

"The old lady I met in my dream, very likely," laughs Jenny.

"You have n't met her or the colonel since that first night, have you, Jenny?"

"No, but I met the nephew they were so anxious to make me marry, last night, and I 'm getting quite reconciled to the match, Martha."

A little more in this gay strain, and then this pretty, brown-eyed, rosy-cheeked "country girl," as she calls herself, trips off on that sight-seeing, social errand which, if the truth were told, brings

more people together in Boston on this famous anniversary week than all the ologies and isms combined. But in spite of her modest disclaimer of
other interest Jenny had a quick mind and an appreciation of some fine things beyond her. And so
on this last day as she sat in Tremont Temple, and
heard the cadences of a far-famed voice, she forgot
her social errand entirely, and listened, if not with
thorough understanding, with great admiration and
the keenest attention. It was in the midst of this
eloquence, and while her attention was at its height,
that a lady acquaintance leaned over from a front
seat and signaled for her fan. As she reached
forward in passing it, a gentleman near her turned
his face towards her. Jenny Merryweather's nerves
were well sheathed, as she had said, under that
firm, healthy flesh of hers; but a very queer sensation thrilled her as she saw that the face of this
stranger — *was the face of the man she had twice
met in her dreams* — the face of the man whom the
old royalist had called his nephew. In the sudden
movement the gentleman had changed his position
and now sat where she had a full view of his lineaments. Yes, there were the same marked lineaments; the high and long nose, the searching, but
at the same time peculiarly drooping eyes, above
which straight black brows and heavy, short-cut
hair gave a resolute look, which the square shaven

chin by no means counteracted. The only sign of
beard was on the upper lip — a thickly-grown,
well-trained ebon moustache. How the famous or-
ator progressed in his discourse after this, Jenny
never knew. But at the end of the discourse, as
she stood waiting to pass out, she suddenly became
aware that those searching eyes were fixed upon
her face with a curious intentness. Friends and
acquaintances approached her, and she responded
to their salutations, and laughed and talked in her
ordinary manner; but all the time she was quite
conscious of her unknown, mysterious neighbor,
quite conscious that he was keeping her in view
through the slow passage to the door. Then, in a
moment, she lost sight of him. She was to meet
Martha that day at the Parker House, where they
were to have a *tête-à-tête* lunch together, and
afterwards indulge themselves in a millinery hunt.
Over that first cup of coffee Jenny told her strange
story of the morning.

Mrs. Martha looked as if all the ghosts of the
ancestral mansion had suddenly appeared before
her. When she found voice from the excess of
amazement it was to say: "Who would have
thought, Jenny, that such a little, matter-of-fact,
practical person as you would have been the heroine of such an uncanny mystery?"

Jenny laughed. Then in a moment, "Martha,

you treat this little sequel to my dream with more respect than you did the dream itself."

Martha colored, glancing at Jenny in a quick, observant way, but made no reply. "And I don't know as I wonder at it," went on Jenny. "Of course, this queer fact of my meeting my dream-gentleman in broad daylight makes the chief interest in the dream itself. But I must say *I* found the dream exceedingly interesting before," with an arch, significant glance at Martha. But Martha, evidently not disposed to discuss this matter, asks abruptly : "Jenny, you said you met this person in your dream last night. Tell me about it."

"Well, there is n't much to tell. I don't remember any events as in the first dream. He seemed to appear before me as if for no other reason but to impress his face upon my memory, or it seems like that now ; for though it made a clear impression in the first dream, it was nothing like the exactness with which every feature and every expression fixed itself like a photograph in my mind last night."

"I never heard anything like the whole affair, never," ejaculated Mrs. Carrique with emphasis.

"*I* have," quietly returned Jenny. "Nothing of the kind, of course, ever came under my own observation or experience before, but I 've read and heard of such things. We 're Scotch folks, you know, on my mother's side, and I 've heard Grandma MacKay tell a great many of those old, second-sight, Scotch stories, and specially about such dreams as mine. A great many of them, I believe, are purely imaginary, helped on by some old tradition, but now and then something like this experience of mine happens to some practical little body like myself."

" I wonder what Frank will say to *this!*" cried Mrs. Carrique, in a sort of triumph.

" *I* sha'n't tell him, but you can if you please."

"Of course I shall," and that very night she kept her word.

Frank Carrique laughed as was his wont. And what he said was not much more encouraging to Mrs. Martha. In fact, he doubted the whole story; believed that Jenny had become so impressed with that dream-gentleman that she endowed the first fine-looking fellow she saw with his lineaments.

"That shows how much you know Jenny Merryweather!" retorted his wife in great scorn. "She 's about as fanciful as you are, — just about. I wish you 'd seen her at lunch while she was fresh from that queer encounter, and relating it to me. It really excited *me* so much that I forgot my appetite. But Jenny!" — and Mrs. Carrique stopped, unable to express herself adequately upon the marvel of Jenny's appetite at such a time.

"I don't think Jenny is very fanciful, myself, Martha, but girls will be girls," declared Mr. Carrique, with the young masculine air of settling the matter by his summing up.

"And stupid men *will* be stupid men," retorted Mrs. Carrique, with a grimace at her lord and master.

Aggravating as all this unbelief was to Mrs. Martha, she took pretty good care not to seek sympathy on the subject from Jenny. Her visit would come to an end now in three days, and she meant that it should end as smoothly and pleasantly as possible. The last night of all, the ancestral mansion was to be turned into a pretty scene of festivity — a farewell party for the two or three guests whose departure would be nearly simultaneous. On the morning of this last day Jenny came down equipped for an expedition to the city again.

"Now, Jenny, what *are* you going to heat yourself up for to-day of all days — the anniversaries are over, are n't they?"

"Yes, but I *must* have new ribbons for my pink dress."

"And so you are going to heat yourself and get red and blowsy for to-night."

"Martha wants you to look your best before her new relations. There 's to be a very strong force of Carriques to-night, you know; and I believe she

has a special design about a certain cousin of mine,
Tom Carrique, who happens to be here now from
Philadelphia."

" Now, Frank " —

" Now, Martha, I 'm not going to have Miss
Jenny taken unawares."

" Jenny, if you believe half that Frank says," —
began Mrs. Carrique, with a little guilty blush.

" I don't," retorted Jenny, laughingly. " I believe only one third, the other two thirds I put
down to pure fancy, following his wise example of
judgment where the opposite sex are concerned ! "
There was a mischievous sparkle in the glance that
this little Jenny darted at Mr. Carrique here, which
winged her arrow straight to the mark.

"Oh ho," thought that gentleman ; " so Mart,
after all, went and told her of my heresy about that
dream-hero of hers."

But Mart had done nothing of the kind, as he
found out later. Walls, it is said, have ears, but
Jenny found not even a wall barrier as she sat on
the door-stone that day and the wind came sweeping every sound to her, far and near. She had
been a good deal nettled, when this accident
brought Mr. Carrique's persistent disbelief to her,
but she had succeeded so well in keeping out of
sight that no one suspected it until this small shot.
Full of wonder, but fearing a little breeze, Mrs.

Carrique turned the conversation by going back to the pink dress.

"Why don't you wear your white tarlatan, Jenny? It would be lovely with a trimming of pink roses and buds."

"Yes, but where are the pink roses and buds, Mrs. Carrique?"

"At `McDougal's greenhouse, my dear. I 've ordered loads of flowers from there and I might as well tell him to send me some roses. Don't you remember that small, perfect, pink rose we saw there the other day. I don't know what variety it is, I never can remember such things, but it would be just lovely for your white dress."

This settled the matter, for Jenny had greater faith in Martha's taste than her own. That night standing before the long mirror in the red room, she suddenly turned to Martha, who was looping the overskirt, with the words: "Martha, you 'll think I 'm cracked, I dare say; but as true as I am standing here, I remember now, for the first time, that I was looking just like this, in this white dress and pink roses I mean, when I found myself standing before the old colonel in my dream. I remember now, that I stood at this very glass before I went down, and regarded myself as I do now."

"My goodness gracious!" exclaimed Martha, dropping a whole paper of pins, in her trepidation.

"You know I told you at the time that the nephew's dress was of the fashion of to-day, but I never remembered my own dress until this moment. This is what you call *a latent memory*, I suppose," and Jenny laughed a little.

"My goodness gracious!" again exclaimed Mrs. Martha, as she picked up her pins, "I believe it all comes of this room, Jenny, and — but there's the bell and I'm not half ready," with which curiously unfinished sentence Mrs. Martha whisked out of the room as if she were fleeing from a small army of ghosts. Jenny looked after her in surprise; and for a moment as she stood there alone and heard the wind sweeping through the long passages, and clicking the old door latches, an undefined feeling came over her, not of fear, but of something unusual, either in the atmosphere about her, or in her own state of mind. "It is all in my own mind, of course, and no wonder after all this queer dream work," she concluded, as she took up her gloves and went down to the drawing-room. Once in that gay, bright room, seeing the pretty reflection of herself in the long mirrors, and meeting an endless array of Carriques in one and two and three generations, she forgot all about the "dream work" and its puzzles, and remembered only the very agreeable present — that she was looking her best, and that Tom Carrique's eyes, as he bent above her, were beaming with a flattering consciousness of that fact. The rooms were rapidly filling with brilliantly dressed people, but her new admirer held his place beside her, as if he intended to hold it for the rest of the evening, and they were both in the full swing of that remarkable nonsense young people delight in, when Jenny's attention was arrested by her host's voice, exclaiming in a tone of great astonishment: " What, you, Henry ! What in the world does this mean ? "

" Don't be alarmed, Miss Merryweather," explained her companion, " it 's only another Carrique; he is n't considered up to the Carrique standard of good looks, but, however, here he comes, so you can judge for yourself."

" I came on in the Europe, and I should have been in to see you a day or two ago, but Morris and Kate wanted me to come out with them and surprise you." This was the answer Jenny heard in reply to Frank Carrique's question, and the next moment the owner of the voice came in sight, and she saw — *the hero of her dream again!* Her gay companion rattled on, and she responded with that sense of perception which keeps the external routine of social life in order under difficult circumstances. But all the while she was watching the new-comer, listening to Martha's cordial reception of him, and holding her breath in a sort of eager restraint till she should be brought face to face with him.

It was at this moment that the tension began to show a little.   Tom Carrique, regarding her with a half-laughing scrutiny, said to her : —

" Miss Merryweather, what is it ? you look as if you had seen a ghost."

" Perhaps I have," she answered, in the same tone.   The next moment she knew that Frank Carrique was standing before her, and was saying in his jovial voice : " Here 's another Carrique, Miss Jenny.   My cousin, Mr. Henry Carrique, fresh from Paris, Miss Merryweather."

Then, almost reluctantly, she raised her eyes, and met the same intent gaze she had received in Tremont Temple three days ago.   As Frank Carrique moved off to speak to some one else, this new-comer, bending forward a little, asked in the quietest way : " Did you like Weiss the other morning?   I believe I saw you at the Temple — you sat directly back of me."

" What an impression my strange staring must have made upon him," was Jenny's uneasy thought at this.   But she need n't have feared.   Henry Carrique was no more vain or self-conscious than herself.   He had not flattered himself by such observance as Jenny had given him.   She had interested him for quite another reason.   It was for this reason, doubtless, that he held his place beside her for so long a time, talking to her in that

same quiet confidential tone with which he had begun his conversation with her.

" Henry has cut me out entirely with your little
school-mistress," whispered Tom Carrique, in Mrs.
Martha's ear, in the course of this "conversation."

Mrs. Martha laughed, but she looked disturbed.
She had always heard vague reports that Henry
Carrique was a very agreeable man, who made
himself fascinating to women with no intentions
of marrying, and although she had by no means
set herself to the onerous task of match-making,
she did n't want her friend Jenny trifled with.
Making a little detour presently she made a little
effort at breaking up the prolonged *tête-à-tête*, but
unsuccessfully. At this failure she beckoned to
her husband.

" Break up that flirtation, Frank, and bring
Jenny over to me. I want her to know the Dunham girls."

" Flirtation ! they are talking about the iron
mines in some Russian town," Frank responded,
with a laugh at his wife.

" I don't care what they are talking about; I tell
you it 's a flirtation, Frank, and I want you to break
it up. I don't approve of such monopolizing on the
part of your cousin."

Frank shrugged his shoulders. He saw how it
was, but like a sensible host — would that hostesses

possessed the same shining virtue — he hated to break up a *tête-à-tête*. "Why can't women let each other alone?" was his inward query; but being a very new husband he felt bound to please his wife at any cost, and so, though much against his will, went forward to do her bidding. It is very curious how a concealed motive will sometimes convey itself to the person or persons most concerned. There was certainly nothing strange in the fact that a pretty girl like Miss Merryweather should be wanted elsewhere, and Henry Carrique was sufficiently a man of society to know that he *had* rather monopolized the young lady; but when Frank Carrique, following his wife, came up with the easy and natural request that Miss Jenny would allow him to introduce her to the Dunham girls, Henry Carrique knew that this was simply a ruse to separate him from his companion. He laughed a little, and thought quickly, "So I 'm warned off, eh?" And, as a matter of course, a new element of interest was added to the curiosity he already felt about his new acquaintance. Jenny, too, as keen, perhaps keener, in her perceptions, made a conclusion not far from the truth, that Mr. Henry Carrique was somehow considered a dangerous person, at least, as far as she was concerned, and so, as a matter of course again, a new element was added to *her* interest. To her there seemed to be a kind of fresh but unseen bond established between them from this fresh circumstance. After this she found it quite. impossible to make a further confidant of her friend Martha — to tell her, what would have been so natural under other conditions, the new fact of identification which had astonished her in the person of Mr. Henry Carrique. But that night, when the guests had all departed, and Frank was putting out the gas down stairs, Martha came into Jenny's room for " a little talk." " Well, Jenny, how did you like my favorite, Tom Carrique ? " was her salutation, in tones of suspicious airiness.

Jenny, the most straightforward of mortals, drives through this manœuvre at one plunge, and with a spirit which Mrs. Martha cannot mistake. " I liked him very well, Martha, but I found Mr. Henry Carrique much more interesting, partly because I saw more of him, I suppose."

" Yes, I dare say, Henry Carrique can make himself very agreeable. He 's a great flirt, you know, or at least people say so. Nobody ever thought he 'd marry, until last year, when he sent home the news of his engagement. He 's acted very strangely about it ; did from the first ; but he 's very eccentric, and as he 's no relative nearer than a cousin, nobody has any particular claim upon his confidence."

Jenny blushed a bright red at this information, but more from the vexation that always assails a person of quick perception when they discover that they are being indirectly warned, and " talked at," than from any other feeling.   Never very prone to restrain that quick spirit of hers, she flashed out here, " Thanks, Martha, for your good intentions, but I don't need your caution, *yet*, at all events ; I 'm not in love with Mr. Henry Carrique."

Martha colored up, the color of the red room itself.   " Now, Jenny, that is so like you."

" So like me to see straight through your transparencies, Martha — I know that," laughed Jenny. " But if you *would n't* beat round the bush with me, Martha ! "

" Yes, if I 'd come at you brutally, and say, ' Jenny Merryweather, Henry Carrique is a dangerous person, and in my opinion will fool you to the top of his bent, and then go off and marry that girl that he is engaged to, and leave you to wear the willow,' I suppose you mean to say that you 'd like that style ·of thing ? " retorted Martha, brought to bay.

Thoroughly restored to good humor by this outburst, Jenny replied, gayly : —

" Like it, I should adore that style, Mart ; I always like people to hit straight out.   I hate anybody to give me little pokes on the sly."

Mart laughed in return, and so the matter passed over, leaving Mrs. Carrique feeling as if she had been rather ridiculously premature, not only in her speech but her fears. But the next day when Henry Carrique walked in with that pleasant, easy manner of his, an hour or so before Jenny's departure, on some flimsy errand about a fan he had unwittingly taken away, Mrs. Martha got back more than her original fears and suspicions. But she would checkmate him yet. He had no doubt come with the design of accompanying Jenny to town on that long horse-car ride, which would take her to the Eastern station. The day was warm, the roads dusty, and Mrs. Martha had a headache, but to outwit this cool fellow, this dangerous schemer, she would gladly sacrifice herself; and so when Jenny rose to take her departure, Martha whipped on her hat, pinned up her pretty, black grenadine that the dust spoiled, and announced that she had concluded to go in to town with her. For a moment Jenny was "unaware" of the "situation," and out of her honest heart protested in this wise. "Why, Martha! it is very good of you, and I should like your company, but you can't get back in time for your dinner at five, you know."

"I intended to accompany Miss Merryweather, if I was happy enough to find her here, that is, if she would permit me," interposed Henry Carrique, in the most matter-of-course way.

Mrs. Martha was breathless for a moment, at this very easy declaration of intentions. However, she held her ground very neatly by improvising business in town, and the clever fiction of her husband's probable delay on this special afternoon.

At this juncture, Jenny, biting her lip to conceal her amusement, met a look from Henry Carrique's laughing eyes, that seemed to establish another little link in the bond between them; and when he parted from her at the Eastern depot, there was a merry kind of intimate acquaintance in their manner which poor Mrs. Carrique little suspected resulted from her own indiscreet action.

Going home, Jenny Merryweather had now two reasons for giving Mr. Henry Carrique the principal place in her thoughts. One, very naturally resulted from the odd dream. The other, the true girl reason of finding great interest in what she had been specially warned against. Mr. Henry Carrique also found himself stimulated to double interest for the same reason, which, after all, it is better to call the human reason, for masculine as well as feminine perversity develops equally in this direction. But Mrs. Frank, dear soul, received no light upon her own share in this business, even when about a month later her husband came home one night with the intelligence that Cousin Henry had joined a certain boating-club at Balem, and that gossip had it that he was very attentive to Miss Jenny Merryweather.

" I shall just go out to Balem in the early train to-morrow morning," cried Mrs. Martha.

" Now, my dear, look out how you meddle with such a matter."

" I shall go out to Balem in the early train to-morrow morning, and do my duty. I know Jenny better than you do, sir, and I know that my words will weigh with her."

" If it was n't for this queer engagement of his, 't would be all right," remarked Mr. Carrique, musingly.

" What ? " from Mrs. Martha, in accents of indignant amazement.

The gentleman repeated his word.

" And you can say that, knowing Henry Carrique to be such an unprincipled flirt."

It was now Frank Carrique's turn to look amazed.

" An unprincipled flirt! Henry Carrique! Where did you get that idea, I should like to know."

" Where *should* I get it ? From you, sir."

" Now, Martha, you *are* such a headlong creature. I told you once that Henry was an odd fellow, and, though very attractive to women, that we did n't consider him a marrying man. You draw the conclusion from that, I suppose, that he is a male flirt. But he is nothing so contemptible. He is n't even much of a society man. He is interesting to men as well as to women."

Mrs. Martha was silent a moment from a little feeling of anger towards her husband, and a little mortification likewise, for she was candid enough to know that her imagination sometimes translated things rather vividly. But presently she says triumphantly: "If this is the case, why do you feel annoyed about your news?"

"For the very simple reason that Henry may be quite unconscious that he may be interesting Jenny unduly. His joining the boating club is n't strange, for he is an intimate friend of Dick Otis, the president."

"It 's a ladies' and gentlemen's club, is n't it, and they go sailing after sunset, by moonlight, and to picnics, and all that sort of thing, don't they?"

"I believe they do, Mart," and Frank Carrique laughed.

"I shall go out to Balem in the early train tomorrow morning, and spend the day with Jenny, and you 'll come out for me in the afternoon, sir."

It was altogether too much trouble for Frank Carrique to combat this positive decision; and it is not unlikely that he felt, himself, the necessity for some sort of action in the matter. However it

may have been, Mrs. Carrique took her own way
after this without further protest from her husband; and the next morning astonished Jenny
Merryweather by her unexpected appearance. But
Jenny Merryweather was a shrewd little person,
as has been shown, and this unexpected appearance led her to thinking at once; and when Mrs.
Martha began to approach the subject of boating
parties in what she fondly supposed a most adroit
manner, Jenny electrified her with: —

"Now, Martha, what is it? You have n't come
all the way to Balem without a special purpose,
and you might as well out with it at once."

Thus it was that Martha Carrique was hurried
into instant and premature confession of her errand.
But Jenny took it all with great external calmness.
"Odd, you call him odd," she said, in answer to one
of Martha's statements; "I don't see anything odd
about him. I can understand him very well."

Poor Martha drew a deeper breath. "Jenny, I
hope you do understand him, for if you do" —

"Don't say disagreeable things about Mr. Carrique, Martha. He is my friend, nothing more, I
assure you. But he *is* my friend; we can like our
friends too well to hear them attacked unjustly,
and you 're attacking Mr. Carrique unjustly when
you accuse him of trifling with me. He has been
very kind and courteous to me. He knew from
the first that *I* knew of his engagement."

Martha could say no more. She felt now that she had said too much in using the word "trifling" as she had. When Frank came up the long, old-fashioned garden-path that night she hastened to meet him, that she might tell him the fruitlessness of her errand. Frank was generous enough not to say "I told you so; I knew you would make a mess of it, my dear."

It was only a few minutes later that the gentleman who was the hero of all this anxiety and commotion walked leisurely up the same garden-path. A bright, interested look came into Frank Carrique's eyes; a look that said plainly: "Ah, now I shall see for myself what everything means." When he saw the expression of Jenny's face, on guard as the poor child was; when he saw Henry Carrique's glance and smile as he approached her, he felt that the meaning was only too evident, and that meaning under the circumstances what his wife had clearly foreseen and apprehended. Perhaps, after all, Martha was nearer right in her summing up of Henry Carrique's character than he had been. As they sat there together on the wide piazza, with the outward appearance of harmony, there was what Edward Everett Hale would have called "an atmosphere" that contradicted this apparent harmony. Henry Carrique was by no means obtuse to this atmosphere, and remembering Mrs.

Frank's previous efforts, he was not far, perhaps, from penetrating its cause. A little ripple of amusement passed audaciously across his countenance, and looking seaward, where a piled up mass of heavy clouds was rising, he said lightly, "There's thunder in the air."

A flash of lightning at this moment sparkled in Mrs. Martha's eyes. She had seen the ripple of amusement, and the words sounded like a challenge. Frank himself was not unmoved, and for the instant a desire to do or say something to the purpose was strong within him. Suddenly, as it seemed, the opportunity was given him. The wind had risen with the rising of the clouds, and a window that fronted the southeast resisted Jenny's attempt at closing. Henry Carrique sprang to her assistance. As he turned back, Frank Carrique held towards him a small, flat, Russia leather case he had just picked up from the floor. The corner was torn off and disclosed a portion of a photograph of a woman's head.

"Yours, Henry?"

A nod of thanks and that same audacious smile again from Henry Carrique.

"That mysterious sweetheart of yours, Henry, I suppose. Come, it is time you told us something further about her, I think."

There was a certain roughness in Frank Carrique's voice, despite his jocular manner. Martha saw — did they all see? — the sudden pallor of Jenny's face at this. Was it the sight of that pallor that produced such a change in Henry Carrique's demeanor? for in a moment his gayety, his lightness, fled, and after an instant of hesitation he seemed to come to a sudden resolution, which cost him a perceptible effort, an effort that brought a tinge of color to his cheek and a new tone into his voice as he spoke. For immediately acting, as was evident, upon this resolution, he moved his chair slightly forward and began : —

"You think I should tell you something further about my mysterious sweetheart, as you call her. I will tell you all that I know myself. About a year ago, when I was in Munich, I received a letter from Kate, containing her usual badinage and speculation, and question, about my prospect of settling in life, as she called it. She said she had heard, through friends in Paris, — the Heydons, you know, — that I was very attentive to a mysterious young Polish girl who had been in society for a short time in Paris. I had met this Polish girl but three times, as it happened, and knew nothing more about her. Just after I had finished reading Kate's letter, I remember I went into Johnny Carew's studio. He was a student in Munich, you know, for two years. On his easel, as I went in, a picture met my eyes that attracted me, for two reasons, the beauty of the face, and the old-fashioned New England look of the dress which the figure was arrayed in. It was a copy he had been making, he told me, of an old miniature he had brought with him, the portrait of his mother's grand aunt, Drusilla Carew. We both of us sat down before this picture and examined it for a while together, and then he went out to keep an engagement, and I sat there for an hour to wait his return, and all the time directly in front of the portrait. I don't mean to say that I was thinking of the portrait all that time: I was thinking of a hundred other things; but I found after I had left the studio the pictured face pursued me. I know I went to a musical party where I met several distinguished artists, but through the talk and the music, and amidst the throng of very pretty women, every now and then I would see in my mind's eye, as we say, Miss Drusilla Carew. It was not very singular then, I suppose, that I should see the young woman again in my dreams that night. The next day I went into Carew's studio, and told him how his ancestress had haunted me. He laughed and remarked: " She's coming back to atone to one of your family, I suppose, for her perfidy in the past." I was all at sea at this, greatly to his surprise, for he supposed, he said, that all the Carriques knew the old family traditions. However, I heard it then and there for the first time from his lips, the old story which I dare say you know, Frank, that a certain Miss Drusilla Carew broke faith, and broke the heart of a Henry Carrique a century ago, or at any rate worked a good deal of mischief with his life."

Frank nodded. "Yes, I know that old story, Henry, but what connection " —

" Has it with *my* story? It is the very root of it, as you'll see, if you have patience. Well, to go on: after Johnny had related the old tradition to me, he produced several photographs that he had taken of his portrait, and allowed me my choice. Evidently, he declared, Miss Drusilla had some interest in me from thus haunting me, and it was but fair that I should possess her picture. So the joke was carried on by his inquiring, when we met, how my phantom sweetheart was. When I wrote to Kate directly after this, the matter being fresh in my mind, I carried the joke along by telling her that at last I had met my fate, but as all things were not as yet satisfactorily settled, though I considered myself an engaged man, I could not yet tell her the lady's name. When Johnny Carew wrote, as he was in the habit of doing now and then, to Kate's husband, he made mysterious mention of painting the portrait of Henry Carrique's sweetheart. So you can see what a fixed matter it became in Kate's mind. Of course, when I returned I intended to confess that it was all jest. Well, I returned in May, as you know. The note in my memorandum-book is, ' Landed in New York, May 23d.' I stayed in New York two or three days before I came on to Boston. The second night, May 24th, I had a curious dream. I dreamed that I was in your house, Frank, not in its present state, but as it was when Grandmother Carrique lived there, the old, unaltered colonial fashion. There seemed to be a great party gathered in the parlor, and I was the centre of it. As I stood there a young girl entered, whose face was the face of Drusilla Carew, but whose costume was that of the present day. Then I noticed that all the rest of the company were dressed in the old Revolutionary style. Only myself and this young girl were in the nineteenth century costume. As she entered I suddenly realized that the occasion was a bethrotal or a bridal, and this young girl and myself were the principal actors. I stepped forward eagerly at this, preceded by an elegant gentleman who was the image of old Colonel Carrique, as he is represented in Stuart's picture. But at this movement the young lady turned abruptly away, and presently, after a few words of remonstrance from the old colonel, she fled incontinently, followed by the colonel himself.

The dream may not seem impressive to you, but it made an odd and fixed impression upon me. Well, this dream, as I said, occurred on the 24th of May. Three days after, I was sitting in Tremont Temple, listening to John Weiss. Suddenly a little commotion took place near me — somebody wanted a fan; I turned and saw in the lady who held the fan the image of Drusilla Carew and of my dream! I believe I may have been very rude in my close observation, and almost pursuit of this lady; but — I hope she has forgiven me" — a half smile here, a quick look at Jenny's face, — Jenny's face which was downcast and colorless, but which with wonderful self-command showed little of the emotion that was agitating her, — a quick look as quickly withdrawn, and then: "Three days or nights after this I went out to your place, Frank, to an evening party, and there I met the lady of my dream, the image of Drusilla Carew, and she was dressed, as I had seen her in my dream, in white with pink roses." He gave another quick look now at Jenny, and then drew the photograph from its case. "Here," to Frank, "you will see for yourself whose face this resembles."

Frank Carrique, with a queer smile about his mouth, regarded the photograph.

"Yes, I see," he said, "and it is not so much wonder. Drusilla Carew was Jenny Merryweath-

er's grand aunt also, or her mother's. If Johnny
Carew had n't been burrowing off there in Ger-
many this half dozen years, he might have told you
that there was a flesh and blood fac-simile of the
old picture down here in Balem in a small cousin
of his. But Johnny's story has another gap in it.
Drusilla, poor soul, did n't break Henry Carrique's
heart, but got her own broken instead. It was a
made up match between the families, and upon
Miss Drusilla rebelling they shut her up in a certain red room in the Carrique mansion — she was
a ward of the old colonel's, and an inmate of the
house until her majority. And here they threat-
ened and persecuted the young woman until she
went into a decline and died there. And ever since
then there has been a story that at certain times,
and to certain persons, these remote people appear
and go through some of their disreputable old pranks
of threatening and persecution. I always thought
this a great piece of humbug, and I do now, but I
must own, Jenny, that all this dream business of
yours and Henry's is as pretty a piece of coincidence as anything I ever heard of. They did appear to Jenny, you know, in a dream, Henry, and —
but I 'm not going to stay to tell you that. It 's
time we were on our way if we are going to drive
home to-night, Mart. The storm is over, you see,
and I 'll bring the horse round." In the little in-

terval of "bringing the horse round," Henry Carrique was wise enough to ask no questions, but afterwards when he found himself alone with Drusilla Carew's grand niece, he asked one question, in the answer of which Jenny Merryweather gave up all the secrets of her heart, all the queer dreams of this strange summer, — gave them up forever into the keeping of her dream's hero, and thus perhaps laid the restless ghost of the red room forever; for it is another queer fact in this queer history, that from that time, from the moment of Jenny Merryweather's betrothal to Henry Carrique, there was nothing further ever heard from the red room; nobody's dreams were ever disturbed by a sight of old lady Carrique's vindictive visage, or Colonel Carrique's blandly cruel face.

"It is a fact, you know, it is a fact, Frank, that lots of people have been worried by that old colonel and his godless old mother when they 've slept in the red room. There was Johnny Carew, and Tom and Mary, and all the Bartletts had a sight of 'em, and now the old thing is done with, and anybody, Carew or Carrique, can sleep the sleep of the just there. You may pooh pooh, and talk till you 're blind, Frank, but there is the fact!" Thus Mrs. Frank Carrique, in answer to her skeptical husband. But skeptical as Frank Carrique is, he can never explain quite to his own matter-of-fact satisfaction the odd coincidence of those "duplicate dreams," as he calls them. It is a subject, however, that he generally avoids, but when drawn into it in family conclave he disclaims all knowledge of details, and has latterly been known to term the whole history, *"One of my wife's stories."*

Henry Carrique, with a less contracted and perhaps more courageous intellect, is quite willing to take Shakespeare's view, that "there are more things in heaven and earth than are dreamt of in our philosophy;" but his little wife, with her Scotch ancestry, beats them all with her belief and unbelief. She scouts at Frank's "timid scoffing," as she calls it; is entirely unbelieving in the theory of coincidence; and believes, as implicitly as Grandmother McKay ever could have done, that she and her husband were brought together by the ghosts of the red room.

"MY NANNIE O."

HERE she is, looking straight down at us with those frank, brown eyes.

"No, they are black!"

Begging your pardon, they are brown — hazel brown. I ought to know, for I have met their rays these thirteen years — ever since I began to think and speculate. Hazel hair too; that prettiest and oddest combination — eyes and hair to match. You can see the color in the curls there, running out over her neck; how could she ever roll it back and submit to that powdering process? Yet it's pretty. The forehead shows its clear brunette tan, the cheeks their rose, "the mouth of your own geraniums red," in brighter contrast for those soft white puffs above them. There's nothing else so different from to-day. That blue silk is fashionable like your own, my lady — a square *corsage ;* and the neck is as white as yours, and the shoulders shaped as finely. Yet she lived almost a century ago.

No wonder you say, " Oh, that those lips had language!" *I* have, hundreds of times, peering into their "own geraniums red," like a bee into a rose, yearning to have some fairy, waft her down with her wand from that painted enchantment, and see her step stately in hoop and farthingale along the gallery. I call it a gallery, though it's only a wide hall, with no grandeur of fresco or carving; but it is hung with these old family portraits — from end to end. If my father had a passion in the world, it was for collecting these painted semblances of his race; and here they are, a motley assemblage enough, "peace to their ashes." Here they are — man, matron, and maid, soldiers, priests, and scholars; and one or two with a ribbon across their broad breasts, starred, and otherwise ornamented with signs of a foreign service. Courtly looking cavaliers, in good sooth, with faces that remind you of those young French heroes whose pictures are scattered all through the history of Napoleon. These are *my* favorites; but my father was fonder of "My Nannie O" than all the rest.

"How came she by that title?"

Wait. I will let her tell her own story. Here is her diary — written with her own hand — that hand whose perfect copy clasps the great fan of pheasant feathers there. Just think, my lady, while you wave and flirt that little sandal-wood bijou, of the cunning dexterity those other small, fair fingers must have exerted in the management of that enormous thing. Yet, as Domenichino said of his early paintings, "It is not so bad after all." You perceive how the baby proportions of the hand are enhanced by its effort to compass the fan's bulky size, and how, in the stately movements, the soft, plumy tips would waft like some sunset cloud between the lovely girl and her adorers. I am not sure, my lady, but she had the best of it. Behind this screen of defense, what chances she held of carrying on a prolonged siege, wherein her coy resistance was charmingly relieved by a bright glance, or a blush now and then flashing out through the plumy pheasant feathers, and setting the suitor's heart in a flame, to be quenched and fired again by the same tantalizing process ! What can you do, *mia cara*, with that pretty toy? You lean your pretty chin upon it in pretty attitudes, it is true ; you tap it lightly against those milky pearls, which stand in rows there between your scarlet lips ; you mockingly raise it before your face in a playful threat ; but "My Nannie O" had but to turn her slim wrist, and build a wall between herself and the sighing swain. Almost a century ago ! What a long, long time !

"And did she live to lose that dimpled smoothness, that bonny brown hair, that rose-geranium color ?"

No; that is the best of it. There is no bowed figure, and wrinkled face, and silver hair, that once bloomed eighty years ago, and called itself " My Nannie O." No, —

" Beautiful Evelyn Hope is dead."

And she is always beautiful Evelyn Hope now to us.

Eighty years ago, then, she was twenty — a rose in bloom. Eighty years ago that fair hand first began to pen

HER DIARY.

June 10, 1795.

To-day I am twenty years old, and to-day I promised to begin a diary — a daily diary to the end of my life. The end of my life ! It makes me shiver ! I wonder when I shall die ! and I am so afraid of that thing called Death — that thing ! Yes, an actual presence. Dr. Parker says I must be very wicked to feel so ; and if I don't repent and love the Lord, that I shall go to hell. His words are mere words — nothing more to me. " Repent and love the Lord ! " He talks as if I had only to *will* repentance and love. Let us see ; what have I to repent of ? Last night, in dancing with Mr. Glancey, I let my glove fall, and when he picked it up so gallantly, and asked to keep it, I pretended a great deal of propriety, and demanded it back again, when

I did n't care a pin for it. Indeed, to tell the whole honest truth, which I will do in this diary, because it is between my soul and I, I would n't care for his keeping it *provided* he had stolen it — 't was a pretty glove, and shaped to a pretty hand! In this, then, I have acted a lie; and I ought to repent of lies. I wonder what Tom's wife would say; I 'll ask her. She 's very decorous and very strict. I shall ask her, — " Jane, what should I have replied to Mr. Glancey, when he picked up my glove in the dance the other night, and asked to keep it?" Jane will look at me in silent amazement a moment; then she will answer, " Why, ' No,' of course!" " What, when I would rather he would have it than not? Would n't that be a lie, Jane?"

Then how she will talk to me. I " must be very corrupt to feel so!" I am not corrupt! I am only natural. When he picked up the glove and asked for it, the thought came, quick as a flash, that it was a pretty thing for him to ask, and that it would be a pretty reminder of me. Then another flash brought up all the Sister Janes and the Aunt Prudences, and I answered " No!" Eh! but what did the naughty Nannie do next? She gave him the flower that had lain on her neck through the evening; and when he kissed the flower and said, " Happy flower, who does not envy thee?" she made him a sweeping courtesy, and sent him a laughing response very softly, so that the Sister Janes and the Aunt Prudences could n't hear!

French women do these things, Jane will tell me, and French women are coquettes. Well, but then I came·honestly enough by it, Sister Jane. There is blood of the *ancien régime* in my veins, you know. Viscount Chastellux, who came over in the French fleet, was mamma's brother. dear; that's his portrait over the fire-place in mamma's room, you remember. He named me, too; and they say I look like him — have his nose and his hair. Only think — that splendid young officer! I am so vain of it my head is quite turned.

There, I had forgotten that I was to confess my sins here on this white paper. Good little page, I 'll call thee a white-robed priest. That's it — I 'll turn Catholic just quietly here, and tell my beads on that pearl necklace De Grémont gave me. Now, down on your knees, Nannie, to confession!

Firstly, I have told a lie. *Secondly*, I stayed away from church last Sabbath because my new bonnet was n't done. *Thirdly*, I got into a passion with Hannah for putting powder on my hair when I told her not, and boxed her ears. That's a pretty story to tell my lovers, eh? I know some of my sweet sex who would relish the telling, though. *Fourthly*, after making *beaux yeux* at young Parson Leighton, I refused him flatly yesterday. *Fifthly*, I went out on Tuesday with my young brother John, and gave him the slip while he stopped to watch the man with the puppet-show; and just at that time Mr. Glancey, whom papa does not favor, came up with me, and we went out on the old road for a walk, and did n't get back for two hours or more. *Sixthly*, when papa found this out by little John, and reproved me with sharpness, I swept him a saucy courtesy, and reminded him that I should never demean my old French blood: his first marriage, before he ever saw mamma, was a *mésalliance* with one of the provincial *bourgeoisie*. *Seventhly*, on going out of the room I encountered little John and scolded him for tale-bearing, shaming him into tears and indignant denials. Whereupon I told him that he should die in silence, if he would be a gentleman, rather than to tell secrets; and I have treated him very cruelly since. *Eighthly*, I refused to ride with Mr. Edward Overing yesterday morning because he chose to give me some advice about my conduct on the night of the ball, telling him I wished there would be another revolution, that we might see specimens of gentlemen here in America such as my mother remembers, and telling him various savage things that I 'll warrant spoilt his sleep that night. *Ninthly*, when my mother asked me to go to Mrs. Overing's this afternoon with the apple-jelly for little Sally, who has the measles, I answered " No ! " very unbecomingly, and said I was tired of the Overings, and would n't wait on them any longer. There was no one else to go then, and I saw her set out herself without a word.

Here 's a list for you, good priest. Which do I repent? Which? Hear that! Well, I don't repent giving Mr. Glancey the flower, nor the courtesy; but about the lie? Oh, I 'm repenting that in sackcloth and ashes! And I don't feel very bad about my bonnet sin, though I suppose that it is because I am so wicked. But I am sorry I boxed Hannah's ears, for it was not becoming a gentlewoman; and Hannah is a good girl, though she tries my temper with her forgetfulness. Then I am not sorry I refused Parson Leighton, for I did n't want him, and I could n't help making *beaux yeux* at him any more than I could help breathing; for he has *beaux yeux* himself without the making, and he is forever following me about. And I don't repent walking with Mr. Glancey, though papa frowns on him. He is a gentleman, though he is a gay British soldier, and a second son; but I am sorry I spoke up to papa as I did — that was mean and cowardly in me to reflect upon his poor young wife, whom he married for love, and who died so soon. And I am sorry I treated little Johnny so cruelly, for the lad is far better than I, and loves me more than anybody or any-

thing, save his romantic notions of right and truth.
As for refusing to ride with Mr. Edward Overing,
I am not repenting much.   He, to set himself up
as my adviser!   For my last offense, I repent most
heartily and honestly, and long to lay it all to the
door of his high mightiness, Edward Overing; for
if he had but held his peace, I should never have
answered my sweet mamma so rudely, and allowed
her to go through the hot sun on that tedious walk.
My sweet mamma, who never said a sharp word to
her disobedient, disrespectful daughter.   But I am
to put it all down to my hot temper — my fiery
Chastellux blood.   I know there is no use in excuses.   I will have no shoulders but my own to
bear this sin.   To-morrow I will do penance.   I
will scourge my willful spirit by spending the
whole day in mamma's service; and it is house-
cleaning day, so it will be bitter scourging enough,
for I hate the whole thing.

So endeth the first lesson of my diary; so, good
little priest, I have knelt at thy confessional.
Bless me in the name of my godfather, who believed in the holy Catholic Church, the saints and
the martyrs.

Saturday, 1795

Well, I knew it would be so.   I prophesied the
very words.   "You must be very corrupt to feel in
this way."   Yet they moved me as if unexpected.

Oh Jane! Jane! in your cold, unnatural presence
I feel so spelled with evil that I can never talk
freely. But what matter? She would not comprehend if I did. And yet she is like most of the
women one sees — so artificial, so afraid to evince
emotion. Even my kind, good Mary, Henry's wife,
looked quite shocked at me one day when I told her
I hoped that I should marry a man I loved sometime ; and more than that, as I declared that I
liked the society of the other sex so much. So do
all women — the little hypocrites !

" Corrupt ! " how the word follows me — how
it angers me. My cheek flames, and yet I know
it is a corrupt estimate. Yes, a corrupt estimate !
Jane is a type of most of the girls I know. There
are the Eldons, the Drakes, and the Cartrights —
how they talk of proprieties ! — how they turn up
their noses (Liz Drake's is such a pug) at some
poor sinner of their sex, whose steps have wandered out of *their* track ! I scared them most to
death one day by reading a translation I made of
La Magdaléne. If I had n't been Judge M'Lean's
daughter they would have flouted *me* — *me*, Nannie
Chastellux M'Lean. As it was, Miss Miriam El-
don relieved her mind by a long rigmarole without
rhyme or reason, on and concerning the sphere of
woman. Then what did they do? They fell to
scandalizing poor little Mrs. De Croix. Such

things as they told — things that I would blush to
repeat; and they relished the telling. Jane was
present, and she joined in the cry! She liked it
too! A madness seized me then. I broke out in
a storm of indignant passion at them. I told them
their minds were fouller than many a lost sinner's
life: that I, who could translate *La Magdaléne*,
would scorn to talk with my own sex what I would
blush for men to hear. Oh, how my fiery Chastellux blood ran over. I exult to think of it. They
were so frightened they turned pale, but they never
answered me — no, not a word. I conquered, as
truth and right must in the end. I came off vic-
torious with the tri-colored flag of *justice, loyauté,
et charité!* Huzza! *Vive la Charité!*

Wednesday, 1796.

'. This morning I sat to Mr. Allston for my portrait. Papa and Mr. Malbone came in in the
midst of the sitting, which relieved me, for I was
fast getting into a fidget; for, as papa truly says,
I do not relish sitting still, or in one place long.
Mr. Malbone came and looked over Mr. Allston's
shoulder at Mr. Allston's request, for they are famous friends; and I heard him say : —

"What a prophetic look you have put into the
eyes; where did you find that lurking sadness?"
"Where, indeed?" and Mr. Allston suspended his

brush to look at me — a perplexed expression crossed his face, and he seemed disturbed. Then Mr. Malbone came and stood beside me, and began telling me of our dear, delightful old Newport — told me strange and wild traditions, till I got to thinking, I remember, of a story mamma once related to us all when we were children ; a story of how my uncle Chastellux was once thrown upon a curious old island not unlike our Newport — though it was in the south of France, and of a picture he brought away — a picture of a lovely court dame, who was banished for some suspected treason from the kingdom to this little, quaint island city, and who pined and pined for her native land, till at last, grown desperate and crazed, she took her life into her own hands, and when one morning my uncle went to pay his respects to her, he found the house in great commotion and the lady lying in state. An old servant put a package into his hands, addressed in a woman’s handwriting to him. In it he found the painted likeness of herself, and a touching farewell, wherein she thanked him for his friendly offices. The likeness was one he had often seen her occupied upon, — one that she had painted herself, — and the last touch had been given but a few hours before the rash act which terminated her existence. It was evident to him that it was the eyes that had received the latest touch, for in their mystical depths he recognized a wild, prophetic light he had never seen before. So strangely and powerfully did this impress him, that my mother said that he never looked at the picture without an inward shudder and devoutly crossing himself, gay soldier and brave man though he was. Papa was displeased that mamma had told us this story — he did not like for us to get such wild notions in our minds, he said.

I was thinking of all this, as I sat there, when I was aroused by an exclamation of Mr. Allston's, "Look at her now, Edward!" And I glanced up to see Mr. Malbone regarding me earnestly. "There, you see where I got the prophetic look!"

Papa came forward from the window where he had been reading a letter, and surveyed the portrait: "My dear, of what were you thinking awhile ago?" I told him readily, and was surprised to see a heavy frown settle over his face, and he uttered his usual word when vexed, —

"Pshaw!" and then, "That childish story has frightened her; get that look off, Mr. Allston, or I shall not know my brave Nan." "I must take another sitting for it; she is too fatigued now, said Mr. Allston." And thus it was arranged that I should go again the next day, which is to-morrow.

Mr. Malbone promised me to finish his story of

Newport sometime, if I would tell him mine — the one to which I alluded to papa. " He is a nice youth, but very young — too young for you, my gay little coquette; so don't be turning the boy's brain with those arch glances," Mr. Allston whispered as I went out. That's the way they go on. I can't say a civil thing to a young gentleman but I am trying to turn his brain. It's all in my blood — this fiery, Chastellux blood, that sparkles and foams like wine — so what can I do? What do I *care?* Yes, what do I care? I am free —free as God made me. Will I sell my birth-right for a mess of pottage? for it comes to that, this putting rein and check on word and look and motion, and perpetually acting a lie as Jane and the rest of them do. No, never!

" She would not dare say such things if she were other than she is — if she were not Judge M'Lean's daughter." I overheard that sly snake, Sue Cartright, say this to Hannah Carroll yesterday. Thank my stars I'm Judge M'Lean's daughter then! And Hannah, dear, kind little Hannah, defends me, and tells my saintly Susan I am not so much to blame, for I was actually educated in a convent — a French convent! What would papa say to that, I wonder!

Ah, but I yearn for *la belle France;* for the gay streets, the *assemblées,* and the warm hearts.

I am only half American. I cannot get used to
their cold, stiff ways ; they are like their cold,
chilly climate. I shrink and shudder under the
influence of both. Ah, it is very *triste* here, very
triste !

Hark ! what is that ? A guitar. Who plays a
guitar ? *Mon Dieu !* can it be De Grémont !

Wednesday, 1795.

A whole week since I wrote here last. How
irregular I am ! Ah *Ciel,* how perplexed one
gets trying to think in two ways ! Ah, that I
had never left *la belle France ;* that I had remained with *ma grande mère !*

But I shall never make a proper diary in this
way. Where did I leave off — a week since ? I
shall begin on Thursday then, the day I went to
Mr. Allston — what am I thinking of ? Shall I
forget the strains of the guitar that moved me so
strangely ? I knew it could be no other than De
Grémont, and I sat spell-bound. I could scarcely
credit my ears ; but when I heard that low, sweet
song of Burns's he always sung to me, —

" And I 'll awa' to Nannie O,"

my heart gave one great bound and I wept. He had
come away from sunny France, away from the grand
court, the palaces, and the people of his name for

me. In that moment I had forgot that I had promised papa but yesterday to retract my refusal to young Parson Leighton. I forgot that I had even fancied, myself, that I liked the young man; for in that moment I knew that but one love, but one passion, would ever have possession of my heart; that the love I had thought time and absence had stifled was only sleeping; that De Grémont was my destiny; and I must give him some sign. What? A happy idea came to me; I caught my guitar — the very guitar he had given me in France — and began playing that sweet old melody from Favart's Opera. I did not dare to sing, but he knew the words well: —

> " Though young and yet untaught,
>   New feelings sway me now;
>   This love I never sought,
>   It came I know not how."

As I ceased he took up the strain and gave me that tenderest of all songs: —

> "Ma mie
>   Ma douce amie,
> Réponds à mes amours,
>   Fidèle
>   A cette belle
> Je l'aimerai toujours."

Then I heard his retreating footsteps, and I sat there quite still till they had entirely ceased.

And he knew me well — he did not linger: ah, he knows everything so well — all the little nice shades of delicacy and courtly breeding. There is none like him here, not one; and I thought he had forgotten me perhaps. And now he has come to seek me. Will papa frown upon him or smile? The French are our friends surely, — the friends of America, — then De Grémont has princely blood, a noble lineage. He is not very rich, but papa is not sordid.

These thoughts, I remember, passed like lightning through my mind, and all night they kept with me in my dreams. In the morning I awoke with a new feeling. Life was no longer stale, no longer *triste* here. While I had been sighing for *la belle France* more than its kingdom had come to me!

I dressed myself with unusual care, for I knew not at what hour he would present himself. I had many fears that he would delay until my appointment with Mr. Allston arrived, for I knew .what French habits were; but *eh charmante!* at just a quarter before ten I heard a voice I knew so well asking at the door for papa. Oh, the sweet southern accent of France, how it thrilled my heart! Then the two tones together reached me from the study; then the tinkling of glasses as papa offered him wine; then — ah then, a message for me!

I ran down with such nervous haste I shook the powder from my hair upon my neck, and then I stayed at the threshold in a little fright of pleasure and pain. Presently I summoned courage and opened the door. A mist came before my eyes, but through it I was conscious of a glance that rapt me from that moment away from the world. Then he started forward to meet me — he took my hand — he murmured softly : — .

"And I see you once more! I have prayed for this hour, Nannie." Here my father interposed : "De Grémont, you know upon what terms you meet !" I heard the words, but they sounded afar off. I did not catch their meaning. I only comprehended De Grémont's reply as he waived his hand with a little gesture as though he put away some obstacle. "Give her to me five minutes, five seconds, Monsieur M'Lean, and then " — I was in some sort of a dream for a space — severed from my common daily life and in a little sphere of rest and delight. Then my hand was released with a lingering pressure ; it was like a farewell, and before he spoke I felt as if the north wind was blowing down to my southern vintage land, and I was once more alone.

"M'amselle," he said, "I have told your father that I love you — that I have good blood, good position, and respectable means. He approves all

this, but refuses you to me because I am of the
Mother Church; because I am not of your faith;
and, m'amselle, he says you are to be given in
marriage to a priest of his order!"

Then I told the whole truth. Was this a time
for faltering? I told of my preference long ago
when we walked in the garden of the old château,
and how it had grown to something deeper now,
and that I could never consent to marry another
man.

Then my father put on his iron look. Ah me!
and as good as swore that I should never marry
one of the corrupt Catholic Church; indeed, that
I should never marry other than young Leighton.
My blood rose at this — my fiery Chastellux blood
— and I said some rash things; and there before
us both he stood, De Grémont, looking like an
angel — so kind, so sorrowful, so calm.

Into my storm of words my father's stern voice
broke again : he never looked at me.

" De Grémont, you know the terms upon which
you meet."

" That I would give her up if I could see her
now — I remember!"

" But I will not be given up!" I cried, in a little
passion of tears. " I will not be given up, De
Grémont!"

Oh the light that came into his eyes, the color

that mounted to his cheek; and I knew then that I had sealed my fate and his. The next moment he was gone; he had wrung my hand at parting, and left a kiss upon it, and a tear — it is my marriage ring. Then my father — how he talked to me — he called me "unmaidenly" and "forward," and sent me to my room with a fire in my heart and rebellion in my soul.

At twelve, when I came down to keep my appointment with Mr. Allston, he stood drawing on his gloves waiting to accompany me. I knew what it meant; I was to be overlooked, watched. I am afraid I have a very bad heart, for I said to myself: "Is this love that my father feels for me, this selfish determination to force me into compliance?" Then I tried to remember how he had in many ways been very kind, and that he was my father and had a right to treat me thus: but I could not *make* it right; the old rebellious heart kept on.

Arrived at Mr. Allston's, we found the door ajar and passed in: two or three persons stood with their backs toward us looking at a picture; and I heard one say : —

"It is the look of those who die young — a sudden, undecaying death !"

I stepped forward — they were standing before my portrait, absorbed in the contemplation. I glanced at papa — he looked annoyed; and beyond

feeling a little wicked pleasure that he had overheard this remark, I did not otherwise think of it.
Afterward, when I spoke of it to mamma, she
shuddered, and begged me not to think of such
gloomy predictions. Somehow it does not trouble
me at all — and I wonder, for I am a superstitious
little thing. Ah, *mon Dieu!* nothing troubles me
now but one cruel fate; and death is better than
separation surely.

I sat a long while to Mr. Allston; but at last he
flung his brush down.

" I do not know why it is," he said, " but I cannot get that look from the eyes: the more I labor
the stronger it becomes."

Papa came round and stood before it with a
disturbed face, glancing at me now and then.
"Your daughter is not well, perhaps, to-day, Mr.
M'Lean?"

"She was never better, sir!" papa answered,
with his coldest manner. "But let it rest a while;
in a week or two the change may come easier."

So we went home and left it, to my great relief,
for I could think of nothing but the strange event
of the morning.

For the next three days I do not think papa had
me out of his sight. On the morning of the fourth
he called me into his study and told me something
that turned me stone-cold — that De Grémont had

sailed for France. “ I saw him last night,” he went on, “ when he intrusted me with this, which I told him I would give into your hands.”   I remembered it — a great seal-ring which had been his father's : a new hope shot into my heart as I took it. The motto was “*Attendre et veille,*” rudely cut upon the shield of gold, and I remembered the old tradition he had once related to me. The ring had been in the family since the time of Louis Quatorze; one of his ancestors had it made for a token — a token of his constancy when separated from the lady of his love — sending it to her by a trusty servant. She understood its meaning, and watched and waited, filled with hope and faith.

I knew that he sent this ring to *me* for the same purpose, and *I* would wait and watch !

That very night, as I sat by the window after every one had gone to church but mamma and I, I heard a low, fine whistle — the same tune, “ My Nannie O !”   He had not gone then; it was all a ruse — a solemn ruse ; no simple cheat of cunning, for he is the best and bravest gentleman that ever lived — a sacred stratagem to overcome the force of might, not right. Mamma was in her room, and I was alone in the parlor ; again the low, fine whistle, nearer yet, under my very window.   I leaned out, I spoke softly : —

“ I am here and alone ; I will come out to you.”

I ran around by the currant path and met him —
met him alone for the first time in three years.
Oh, well I remember that parting in the garden of
the château! — well I remember how he looked as
he said, " When I am my own master, Nannie, I
shall ask you of your father; but you will forget
me ere then, perhaps." And in all the three years,
because I had no word or token, I thought *I* was
forgotten instead. I little understood his sense of
honor and delicacy.

And now he had asked my father the fatal question — fatal it had indeed proved; and here we
met, the scions of the houses of De Grémont and
Chastellux, in secrecy and trepidation.

He asked me to fly with him; he said, and my
heart — ay, my conscience — tells me truly, that
we have no right to sacrifice ourselves to unjust
prejudice and force. He told me of the letter my
grandmother had written to my father — a letter of
approval, giving her consent, her benediction on
our union. And for a question of belief in certain
creeds this union must be denied and given up; ay,
worse — I must enter into a marriage without love,
and while my heart is another's! Ah, *mon Dieu!*
what shall I do. A marriage without love is in-
famy; I would die rather, for I know what love is
now. Thus three days have I been tortured and
fluctuating; every hour dreading discovery of De

Grémont's stolen stay in the city, and to our evening interviews. To-night must witness my decision. Disobedience to my father, or a living death for years perhaps.

What next shall be recorded upon these pages I marvel. Mutiny or death? I shudder and turn cold.

Friday, 1795.

I have decided; last night, while the guests were assembled at Governor Adams's, I stole out in my gauze dress to the old pine avenue, where I had appointed to meet him. He was waiting for me: oh, so worn and haggard in these few days, yet looking so patient and kind! I put my hands in his; I said :—

“ Armand, I will go with you — I am yours ! ” He did not burst out into any extravagance of joy at this. He took it solemnly and still ; for he feels with me that it is a' sad and solemn thing we are to do. Solemnly and still, with hands clasping mine and eyes that grew misty with emotion, he looked down upon me and said : —

“ God give me grace to make your happiness, Nannie ! ”

Then it was arranged for our departure. On Saturday night at eleven a French vessel is to sail for Toulon. He knows the captain, the officers — they are friends, every one. There is a chaplain, too — the old chaplain of the château — who will marry us. All this time they have waited for us, the good, true people.

After this interview I had to go back to the gay rooms, to answer inquiries as to my absence, and play my part in the scene. I thought we should never get away. The hours were endless, and all night I dreamed of my coming trial, yet deliverance. . . . .

It is now seven o'clock; in three hours I go to meet thee, my beloved. Three hours, and I cut adrift from my father's house forever! Ah, will he curse me? He was never very soft, very gentle, but he must have loved me. I remember once when I was ill how he walked with me all night, a peevish, crying child, in his arms. I remember — God stay such memories! Oh, Lamb of God, give me consolation in this trying hour; soften my father's heart to me! And my mother, my dear French mamma, she will not utterly hate me for this act. She has *merci*, she has *charité*. She loves her race — the people of France; she will have faith in me to the last. She knows I do not demean myself by an alliance with the house of De Grémont. And little John — God bless thee, little John! — thou lovest me, *mon frère ;* and I, oh, Jean! Jean! I may never see thee again!

Ten minutes of the three hours gone. I will

write to the last, and leave this poor brief record
of my New England life behind me, a better explanation than I could now give for my flight.

Brief record, indeed, and offering what vivid con-
trasts! With what lightness I began it, with what
tragic sorrow do I end it! How life, in one night,
from a folded bud became a perfect flower!

How slow the minutes creep! Yet ah, *mon
Dieu!* each one hastens me forever from my father's house. My father's house! To-morrow it
will be all over. He will know what I have done,
that I have fled from his roof and taken the actions
of my life in my own hands! To-morrow! Oh, my
father, forgive me! See! I leave a kiss for you
on this insensible page — a kiss and a tear; and
mother, my sweet French mother, you will say a
prayer for me each night, and I for thee shall never
cease praying! And little Johnny, little Jean, I
have thee in my heart *mignon;* while it beats it
will never turn cold to thee. Ah, Johnny, little
Johnny, thou art all the child left now. Be brave
and gentle, little Jean; and intercede for me, if
hearts are hardened to me when I go. And Jean,
when thou gettest to be a man, do not judge me
harshly and by the world's judgment. Believe that
I acted not hastily, but with calm consideration;
and remember I loved thee, Jean, to the end!....

The wind is rising — how it soughs round the

pines and maples ! Ah, and there is lightning over
the hills.   A storm is coming down to us.   Well,
it is fit, my beloved, for this wild and troubled departure !

How the time goes ! thoughts grow leaden, and
I write but slowly as the hour approaches.   Something tells me I shall never look upon thy face
again my father, nor hear my mother's voice, nor
kiss the lips of little Jean. Never again ! Perhaps
this storm may find a shroud for us.   Ah, how the
eyes of the portrait flashed upon me then.   They
are unchanged as he left them. " The look of those
who die young — a sudden, undecaying death ! "
Is this my fate ?   Am I going now to meet it ?
Well, I would not turn back.   I go to meet it
calmly.   The time approaches — is now here. Farewell father, mother, little Jean — I go with your
images in my heart, and love for you for evermore
in my soul.   Again, *adieu !* . . . .

In family archives and town records there is a
story told of a fearful night in July, 1795, a night
of storm disastrous on land and sea.   Many vessels
went to pieces on the rocks and in the wild winds.
Many sad stories were told of shipwreck and loss ;
but the saddest of them all was of the French ship
L'Esperance.   Not fifty miles from shore the storm
burst upon her in its sudden fury, dismantling sails

and driving her against the rocks, where one bolt of lightning finished the work of destruction. Guns of distress, fired at short intervals, brought the citizens from their beds down to the harbor.

On that night Judge M'Lean, contrary to his habit, was singularly wakeful and restless; he had retired early as was his wont, and, waking after a brief slumber, heard the wind rising and soughing round the pines and maples. A little later a door slammed with violence! How high the wind must be! did his wife hear it? he asked. Yes, she had heard it, too. Just then the dog howled beneath the window — a wild and mournful expression of dumb emotion. Then for a brief period there was a lull; the wind sank away, and the air grew still and brooding.

Slumber again came to the Judge, held him perhaps for an hour, when an awful crash, as if the heavens were rent asunder, awakened him. He started from his bed, flung on his dressing-gown, lighted a candle, and looked out into the hall; he was not a nervous man, nor given to imaginings, but it seemed as if above the raving wind he heard the voice of his daughter Nannie calling in dire distress. He listened — again through the wide, old hall, and down the stairway once again, with tender supplication, the sweet, young voice called "Father!"

He waited no longer, but more rapidly than he had moved perhaps for many a day he strode on to her room. The door was open, a candle flaring low in its socket, and the bed unoccupied. Open on the table lay the " Diary." A few words, and he knew the truth. Yet her voice! Ah! she had repented at the eleventh hour and turned back. She was waiting at the door for pardon and admittance. He would give her both: and the great oaken door was unbarred for the penitent; but only the rain claimed admittance — the rain and the wind. In vain he shouted her name and waited for a reply. None came.

Suddenly the minute-gun boomed through the night: once and yet again ; and once again from afar, borne down it seemed over sea and shore, that sweet, thrilling voice calling " Father ! "

Who may tell what strange, unusual promptings of the spirit stirred within that stern breast as out into the raging storm the Judge, obeying that call, took his way?

Only one boat crew dared to put out on that tossing sea, and that, after the stirring appeals of one who did not belong to their number; and when they pushed off from shore, at the helm there he sat, eager and watchful and still — the old Judge. Returning, they brought the freight of death. Lashed together on a floating spar, hand clasped in hand, and tresses mingling, were the dead bodies of Armand de Grémont and Nannie Chastellux M'Lean.

Long after, the sailors told how the stern old Judge sat rigid and motionless watching the pale, cold face of his dead daughter, and now and then saying softly, " Poor little Nannie ! "

Long after, my father, the last of the old house of M'Lean, brought out of manifold wrappings the portrait of the Judge's daughter. The picture being stained with mildew and must, in many places, he had it retouched. When the painter returned it, the wild, prophetic look that once baffled the unerring brush of Allston was no longer there ; the painter of another age had sacrilegiously stricken it out. But on twilight eves in July, when the wind is soughing through the pines and maples, looking into the lovely face there, I think I see the old, old gleam of prophetic intelligence ; and I say, softly, " The look of those who die young — a sudden, undecaying death ! " Then I only recall the heroine of the French ship *L'Esperance* — Nannie Chastellux M'Lean. But when the sunshine of high noon streams down the hall I recall the arch young girl who scolded Hannah and swept a saucy courtesy to the gay British soldier. But in her tragic hour, as in her gay young life, never a truer, tenderer heart ever beat in womanly bosom than in the breast of " My Nannie O."

IN A STREET CAR.

I.

JIM MALLORY came swinging on a half-run round the corner of State Street to catch an up-town car. "A red car," his friend Saxon had told him; and there it went full speed out of sight just as he came in view of it. An east wind was blowing, as it generally *is* blowing in Boston, and Jim Mallory shivered, and sneezed, and drew up his coat-collar, while he anathematized the Hub of the Universe and her east winds, as a Gothamite was bound to do. Presently, what with the dust in his eyes and the well-known delightful regularity of that city, Jim got " turned round," as the country folks say, and for a few minutes could n't tell for the life of him which was up town or which was down town.

"Confound the place!" he began, when all at once it seemed as if all the cars in the city suddenly appeared. There they were, red cars and green cars and blue cars, bearing down upon him in swift confusion. He hailed the first, and shouted where he wanted to go. The driver shook his head, and pointed backward in the most indefinite manner; and there were six cars behind him.

He hailed the second, and went through with the same humiliating experience. He hailed the third, he hailed the fourth, and all at once came to his senses at the fifth, and discovered they were every one going the wrong way, and he himself all out of the way on the wrong street. He breathed an exclamation more emphatic than polite, and dashed through to Tremont Street just in time to catch the car he was after. Jim was a handsome fellow, ordinarily, but you never would have suspected it now. To begin with, he had a cold in his head; and for

> "A cold in the head
> What can be said,
> Uglier, stupider, more ill-bred?"

Being a blond man, too, made it worse, as every blond, be they man or woman, can testify; for flushed and swollen eyelids and excoriated nostrils show off to most dismal disadvantage beside a blond's "hair of yellow or beard of gold." And then the thin tissues, the light skin, which evinces every disarrangement! Well, besides a cold in the head, Jim Mallory was covered with dust from his head to his feet. Then, *because* of the cold in his

head, he had drawn his coat-collar up around his
ears, and, because of a general uncomfortable condition, he had drawn his shoulders nearly up to his
ears. Then something had happened to his hat.
I don't know what it was. *He* did n't know what
it was, or he never would have sat there right in
the face of those five girls, looking like such a
Guy, without trying to remedy it. It was something between a crush and a twist, which, taken together with his general muffy appearance, gave
him the aspect of a forlorn and seedy old fellow at
odds with himself and with the world. This was a
climax for a young man who led off the *German* in
Avenuedom, and who was spoken of usually by all
feminine Avenuedom as "so *distingué!*" And
there sat those five girls, without a suspicion of
these facts in his history. Five girls as pretty as
girls need to be, laughing and chattering like —
like — well, like five girls. I don't think there is
any comparison that will serve as well as that after
all. There they sat, laughing and chattering, perfectly heedless of the forlorn and seedy old fellow
doubled up in the opposite corner. Such things as
he found out! For there was nobody else in the
car but another forlorn and seedy old fellow at the
end of the seat. And what heed did these girls
think would be given to their chatter by these forlorn old fellows?

"How *do* you get your hair into such a lovely fluff?" inquired a brunette of a blond.

"Why, I roll it up into curls, and then just pass a coarse comb through it. But yours is lovely, too, I'm sure. How do you do yours?"

"Roll it on a heated slate-pencil."

"Oh, but that hurts the hair so. I put mine into crimping-pins," said another.

And still another: "I braid mine and press it."

And still another: "Common hair-pins, I think, are the best of all. But then one looks so like a fury in any pins."

Then the brunette gave a little giggle.

"Oh, girls, I put *my* hair into pins once — those great crimping-pins Lou uses. It was one morning when it rained, and I thought I was safe from visitors. I was going to the opera in the evening, and I wanted to look very nice, you know. Well, there I sat in the parlor, practicing my last singing lesson, and never heard the bell nor a footstep until some one crossed the threshold. Who *do* you suppose it was?" And the little dark head buried itself in a little Persian muff to smother another giggle.

"We *can't* guess. Who was it?" burst out the other four voices in the greatest excitement.

Up came the head from its temporary hiding, the pretty face all a-blush, the dark eyes all a-dazzle

with laughter, the frizzed hair a little the worse for
the Persian muff.

" Oh, girls ! it was Will Hess with Langford —
Langford just home from Paris, you know ! "

" What *did* you do ? " from the chorus of four.

" Oh, I did n't die, and I could n't run away ; for
there they were, right before me : so I made the
best of it, and laughed, for it *was* funny, and then
I snatched our George's Scotch cap from the table
where he had flung it that morning, and covered
up my steel horns and my ugliness in a twink-
ling."

" Plucky, I declare ! " muttered Jim Mallory,
inside of his coat-collar.

" Will said I *deserved* a *Cap*taincy for my coolness and strategy.　Will is always making his bad
puns, you know," concluded the fair speaker.

And then the others took up the tale, and not
one but had some gleeful misadventure to relate.
And in this relating, what mysteries of rats and
mice and waterfalls, of knots and coils and curls
and crimps, were not revealed to Jim Mallory as
he sat there unsuspected in his corner !　It was as
good — no, it was a great deal better than a play
to him.　But presently the car filled, and the heedless voices hushed, and the play was over.　And
presently appeared the conductor, and Jim began
rummaging his pockets for change.

"What! No money! Where in thunder is my pocket-book?" he almost said aloud.

His pocket-book was gone, probably picked when he was frantically hailing those six cars. Yes, his pocket-book was gone. But he must have some loose change about him, certainly! and with all the blood in his veins rushing up into his face, Jim Mallory continued his search — a fruitless search, for not a penny, even, could he find.

Here was a, pretty fix for a man to be in. A stranger, too; and just then Jim caught a sight of himself in a little pocket mirror he had turned out with other effects in his searching, and discovered what a forlorn-looking object he was, and, consequently, how much more difficult and disagreeable was his position!

What upon earth was he going to do? What upon earth was he going to say? He had a quick brain, usually fertile in expedients, but the ignominious facts of the present case were too much for him. He had heretofore declared, with rather a grand manner, that a man should rule circumstances; and here were the most contemptible circumstances ruling him with a rod of iron. "If it was n't for those five girls, now!" he thought. But he might as well have said: "If it was n't for that conductor!" and a great deal better, for there he was, slowly but steadily making his way toward

the lower end of the car, with a wary eye for all
whom he caught napping or negligent.   And there
were those five girls with their tickets fluttering
in prompt readiness!   All at once at this juncture
he became conscious of a pair of the softest, tenderest eyes he had ever seen fixed upon him with a
look of shy commiseration.   It was one of those
five girls.   It was the brunette, who curled her
hair over a slate pencil, and dramatized her disha-
bille.   So, she had been watching him.   She had
seen his empty pockets, and was moved to pity
thereby, spite of his forlorn and seedy appearance.
He felt the blood go tingling up into his face again,
but before he had time to know whether he was
glad or sorry there was a pull at the bell, the car
stopped, and two or three people were getting in.
In the crowd and the confusion up started the
little brunette, and nodding over her shoulder at
her companions, made a hurried rush for the door.
Jim Mallory, sitting there, saw once more those
pitying brown eyes, and then, as her garments
brushed past him, he felt a little ungloved hand
thrusting something into *his* hand.   His fingers
closed over this " something " mechanically.   For
a moment he could see nothing in the hurry and
confusion, but there was a near, faint scent of early
violets, which suddenly vanished with a soft rustle
of silk.   He looked up then, and she was gone.

He looked down — and there in his palm was — "Why, bless my soul, a car-ticket!" as Jim himself exclaims whenever he tells the story. And to follow Jim's words at this point, which will tell the story better than anybody else's words: "There had that little angel, under the disguise of crimped hair and a lot of other nonsense, taken note of my misfortunes, and made her little plan of relief, which she carried out. like the strategist she was, at the very climax of my desperation, and when the stir and confusion about us would cover every movement. Was n't it splendid, though? How many girls do you suppose would have done that for such a muff as I looked to be that day? For I tell you, Tom," — this was to Tom Saxon, — "that I did look something awful. What with those confounded cotton-samples from your office sticking to me, and the dust, and the cold in my head, and a smash in my hat, I was about as seedy a specimen as you ever saw." And Tom thought he might have been.

But out of one dilemma Jim Mallory had stepped fairly into another. As that "little angel in crimped hair and a lot of other nonsense" stepped out of the car, after the performance of her impulsive action, — which was really a very pretty action, — something entered Jim's heart which he had no will nor wish to banish; but, as

I say, it was out of one dilemma into another—
"out of the frying-pan into the fire," Tom Saxon
would laugh, for all the clew he had was a name
that hundreds of girls in Boston owned.   And the
way he got this was at the moment of her vanish-
ing, when the astonished four cried out in chorus, —

"What's Molly getting off here for?"

In vain Tom had brought him face to face with
some half a dozen Mollys of his own acquaintance.
From each, Jim Mallory had turned with a sigh of
disappointment.   Not one of them belonged to his
angel in crimped hair.

II.

It was curious how often after this Jim found
it necessary to visit Boston.   There was always
some "business for the firm," which made it absolutely incumbent upon him to see Saxon & Co.
And when he was there he fell into the habit of
sauntering down Tremont Street about shopping
hours.   And from there to Washington Street,
into Williams & Everett's, or Loring's library.
And not only there, but into trimming stores, into
jewelers' shops, into fancy-goods stores, into cars
and omnibuses, and everywhere that he caught
the glimpse of a little figure with dark, crimped

hair tucked under a morsel of a bonnet. He passed the winter in this hunt. It was worse than the search for change that lucky and unlucky day when he first met her ; or, as Tom Saxon jeeringly said, it was like that ancient search for a needle in a hay-mow. Such a reputation as he got, too, for the most impudent starer decorous Boston ever saw!

"I think that New York friend of yours is horrid, Tom," said not less than six girls that winter to Tom Saxon.

"Horrid! how?" asked Tom.

"Why he follows you about and stares so!"

Tom looked at them. *Every one had dark hair, and every one had it crimped.*

"He came into a car where I was one day," said one of these girls, "and just took an inventory of my features; and then, after fidgeting about two or three minutes, he dashed out."

Tom gave such a laugh at this that the fair speaker looked at him in wonderment, and privately told an intimate friend of hers afterward that she had reason to think that that Mr. Mallory was having a very bad influence upon Tom Saxon, for she had seen him "when — well — when he seemed very unlike himself, to say the least!"

If Tom could have heard this I think he would have laughed still more. As it was, his laugh was

all at Jim Mallory; and Jim himself, though quite
in earnest in his Quixotic search, saw the joke as
readily as Tom, and, with ineffable *bonhomie*, enjoyed his own absurdity.

As I say, he passed the winter in this hunt, and
by spring the excitement seemed to have subsided,
or, at least, to be externally overlaid by other
things. Tom Saxon thought it had died out entirely until one day, as he was strolling across the
Common, listening to some business suggestions of
Mallory's, he saw Jim give a sudden start as a little
dark lady passed, with her hair *crêpé* and a gay
voice, chatting volubly to her companion.

"Jim, I thought you had dropped that string."

·Jim laughed, and sung, in a low baritone, —

"Her bright smile haunts me still."

That was the last that Tom heard of the subject until — well, we will not anticipate.

Winter passed, and spring had come; and with
the spring, premonitions of cholera. All the Mallory family, mother and sisters, were in a state of
worry and fuss from the first, about this expected
scourge. They had twenty plans in twenty days
as to where they would go, and what they would
do. Cape May, and Long Branch, and Newport
went by the board, because somebody had told
Mrs. Mallory that the sea-coast would be unsafe.

Then came all the mountain resorts. This was too far, that was too near, another too full, etc., etc., until a queer little place, perched up among the Catskill Mountains, was decided upon.

"And it will be so nice for you, James dear, for you can get your mails twice a day," said Mrs. Mallory.

But "James dear" made no reply to this. He had other plans.

"I 'm not going to sacrifice city comfort another summer for one of those mosquito haunts," he said to his partner. "And as for cholera — bah!"

And so it came about that, for the first time in six summers, Jim took up his head-quarters in the deserted house at home, and found it, as he declared, the coolest and most comfortable summer resort he had known for a long time, I don't mean to say that he took no excursions away from the brick and mortar and marble. There was scarcely a week but found him for a day or so at one or another of the pleasant spots about New York, which were easily accessible to him by night trains or steamers. In the mean time his mother and three sisters wrote him frantic letters from the Kauterskill. They offered him every inducement they could think of — plenty of room, pure air, a nice table, and "*such* pleasant society."

"The Caledons — most delightful people — are

here," wrote Kate Mallory; "two charming daughters and a son.   They live on our street at home, too; is n't it funny we came way up here to find each other out?"   And here followed an urgent entreaty to brother James to come up by Saturday night without fail and get acquainted with these delightful people.   But brother James had made a partial engagement to go home with Mr. Wing, his partner, on Saturday night, and he did n't "see that he could get away from it," he wrote back to Kate.

Before Saturday night, however, Jim Mallory found it the easiest thing in the world to get away from his partial engagement with Mr. Wing.   It was Tuesday when he wrote to Kate.   On Wednesday morning, as he was walking down the street on the shady side, he suddenly heard a strange, shrill voice call out — "Molly! Molly! Molly!" He laughed a little at the remembrance this called up, and turned to look in the direction of the voice. There was n't a soul to be seen within speaking distance.   But still that voice went on: "Molly! Molly! Molly!" ending with a curious chuckle of laughter.   He turned more quickly this time, and there, just above his head, discovered a gray parrot swinging in its great gilded cage.   He laughed again, and the parrot took it up with his mocking chuckle, and with, it seemed to Jim, actually a

knowing wink at him, repeated once more: " Molly !
Molly ! Molly !"

Jim Mallory shrugged his shoulders, then thought
of the little dark-eyed angel of his search, and was
half a mind to lift his hat to her name, even when
thus shrilly cried, when all at once something appeared at that window by which the parrot swung
which rooted his feet to the pavement.   This
" something " was a little dark, dark head, crimped
and curled, and decorated with brilliant little bows,
that fluttered in the morning breeze like the pen-
nons of his hope.   IIe had spent a whole winter
hunting for her.   IIe had haunted Boston streets,
and Boston cars, and Boston shops, day in and
day out, without result ; and here at last he found
her — here in New York, in the very heat of mid-
summer !

And there she stood, talking and chattering to
her bird, looking more like a little angel than
ever ; and there below, looking up at her, stood
Jim Mallory in a dazed and hopeless condition.
It is n't possible for any young woman to remain
long unconscious of such a gaze as this — some
attraction, magnetism, or whatever it may be,
makes them " aware " at length.   So presently the
owner of the frizzed hair and the fluttering bows
ceased talking to her bird, and, with a little start,
became conscious of the observation of Jim Mal-

lory ; and once observed by those bright eyes, no young man could have had the hardihood to have remained at his post.

But I must say, Jim Mallory left his position gallantly — some might have said audaciously — but there is no audacity but of impertinence, and of this there was not a particle in Jim. So now when he met those bright eyes, and turned away with his hat lifted to them, I say he did gallantly, and the young lady who was the object of this gallantry was intuitive enough to think so too.

You may be sure that as he went he was not so dazed but that he sent a keen glance toward the door which shut in his little dark-eyed lady. But there was only the number 2767 — no betraying door-plate gave him further clew. This was enough, however, for the present. More than enough you would have said if you had watched him that morning. Wing, who was the sedate father of a family, catching the look in his eyes, asked him, with grim humor, if he had lately come into the possession of his Spanish estates.

Mallory laughed his genial, jovial laugh, and confessed that he had had direct news of them.

Fate, which had been so elusive with him for the last six months, now seemed to smile invitingly, for that very night as he paced slowly up the street, humming to himself " Her bright smile haunts me still," there from the doorway beamed the very smile he was singing of — but — but — who the deuce was that — that black-bearded, Italian-faced individual, who sat so composedly on the second step ? What if Jim saw his Spanish estates disappearing in a blue mist at this *if*.

The next moment the mist cleared.

" Mr. Langford, when do you return ? " the lady asked of the black-bearded.

Jim never heard the answer. What did he care when he returned ? he was only " Mr. Langford " to her.

The next sentence brought the blue mist back a little.

" Will says he should like to spend every winter in Paris."

Will? who was this Will? what relation did he bear, confound him, to the dark-eyed little party ? Then he recalled the Will Hess of her gay misadventure. So here he was again. Suppose now this Will Hess had long ago taken possession of his Spanish castle ? Suppose — but hark, what name is that ? Can he believe his ears when Langford says : " Miss Caledon " ? Miss Caledon ? Kate's Miss Caledon ? Yes, clearly, Kate's Miss Caledon, for presently she remarks about the Kauterskill, and something else, which explains her presence in New York for that week. Kate's Miss Caledon ! Was there ever anything like it ?

" What an idiot I 've been ! " he soliloquized. " Rushing all over Boston, when if I had had my eyes open I dare say I might have met her a dozen times on Broadway. Visiting at the Hub with those four girls, I suppose, when I saw her."

Which conclusion of Jim's was the most accurate one he had arrived at for some time, as he ascertained when he called upon Molly Caledon the next morning. Yes, he actually called upon her, upon the strength of Kate's last letter.

To Molly Caledon this call seemed by no means hasty or singular, for after the manner of young women, she and Kate Mallory had become bosom friends in these last six weeks, and what so natural as "dear Kate's " brother calling upon her when she was in town ? I think Kate herself would have been no little astonished if she could have listened to Jim's free reference to her letter ; and I think she might have been doubtful whether she had ever written that letter. Certain it is that Miss Caledon received the impression by this sketchy reference of Jim's, that it was at Kate's information of her presence, and at her suggestion that he ventured to call. But as I have said before, what could seem more natural than this call ?

And what more natural than Mr. Mallory's returning with her to the Mountains? And what more
natural than that on this journey these two should
progress very rapidly in their acquaintance with
such a mutual foundation of intimacy and interest
as " dear Kate ? " As for " dear Kate," she had
the wit and tact to keep her astonishment within
proper bounds, but whenever she found Jim alone
did n't he have to take it ?

"I can't imagine how you can be contented to
stay here, Jim " she would say ; "and I can't
imagine how Mr. Wing can do without you so
long."

But Jim could imagine, and so I think after a
time could little Molly Caledon ; and so I think
after a time could every member of the house ; and
it was n't very difficult to prophesy the *dénouement*
either, in the estimation of these on-lookers. But
to Jim it seemed much more difficult, for Molly
Caledon was far too bright to carry her heart on
her sleeve, and a spice of feminine coquetry helped
her to play a game of hide-and-seek.

There came a day, however, when she had to
give it up, and acknowledge herself found, if not
caught. It was the day Will Hess and Langford
came. " Now, or never ! " thought Jim Mallory, as
he watched her greeting with the aforesaid gentlemen. " Now, or never ! " I think Molly must

have had a suspicion of his design, for with a queer, coquettish perversity she put him off, first with croquet, and then with a very animated discussion with Langford, and so on, through a list of employments and occupations that continually necessitated a third party. But Jim was too sharp for her at last. The mail had just come in, and as he read his letter from Wing with this item at the close: "One of us will probably have to go to Paris next year;" a bit of strategy suddenly proposed itself to him, which he forthwith acted upon. Walking straight by the group wherein Miss Caledon stood talking animatedly with Langford, he glanced up from his letter with the most absorbed air and inquired of the landlord when the next train left.

"Oh, are you going to New York, Mr. Mallory?" asked Molly, with great *sang-froid.* "And if you are, will you undertake a commission for me?" and Molly came forward from the group at this.

Then she saw his serious *preoccupied business face.*

"No bad news, Mr. Mallory?"

"Oh no, not in the least; only my partner writes that one of us must go to Paris; and I suppose that one will be your humble servant. How many commissions shall I execute for you there, Miss Caledon?" looking straight into the pretty face before him. There was a quiver of the eye-lids — a quiver of the lips, and a sudden forgetfulness of the hide-and-seek game altogether ; and Jim knew that he had won.

"Come into the garden, Molly," he said, in a lower tone. "I 've something else to tell you."

They went into the garden, and so absorbing was the story that he had to tell that he forgot all about the "next train" until Molly, as she heard the shrill whistle of the locomotive, looked up slyly into his face, and said : "How about the cars, Mr. Mallory ? I think you 've lost them ! "

Jim laughed. "But I 've found something better than the cars, Molly." And then he laughed still more. And then he told her that other story of the cars when he had first met and fell in love with her.

"And you don't mean to say that *you* were that old codger in the corner ? " asked Molly in amaze.

"I do, Miss Molly."

"My ! but did n't we girls go on ? "

"I should think you did. I found out all your hair-dressing secrets — all about the crimping and frizzing, you know — and say, Molly, do you 'do' your curls now over a slate-pencil ?

and do you ever get caught in your hair-pins by such young gentlemen as Hess and Langford now ? ”

“ My goodness, *did* I go on like that ? ”

“ Just like that ; and I thought the story in the end of the Scotch cap was rather a plucky climax. And when I listened to it, and saw what a gay little bird of Paradise you were, I had no idea that such a tender heart lurked beneath.”

Molly laughed a little and blushed a little as she said : “ Well, I don’t know how any one could have seen another in such a horrid dilemma without doing something to help him out of it. I remember, though, how scared I felt as I jumped up ; for, you know, I had to get off there to hide the action, for I knew *I* should feel silly enough, and I knew it would be terribly embarrassing all round.”

“ Yes, and in that way I learned your Christian name ; for all those four girls wondered what Molly was getting off there for.”

“ And that was why you stopped under my window, Sir, was it, when my bird called Molly ? ”

“ Oh, you saw me at once, did you, Miss Molly ? ”

“ I saw you lift your hat to me, Sir,” answered Miss Caledon, rather confusedly.

" And Molly, my girl ! " returned Jim Mallory, now dropping his gay tone, " I shall lift my hat always to the angel in your nature I discovered that day in the street car."

MRS. F.'S WAITING-MAID.

WHEN General Butler was in New Orleans, Colonel F. with his wife and family occupied the confiscated mansion of a Mr. Chesang — a Frenchman by birth, and a rebel by principle. There were Mrs. F. and her two children, Tom and Eva, — a boy and girl of fourteen and eleven, and Mrs. F.'s sister — a young lady of twenty. Besides these, two or three officers made it their home with them. It was a pleasant party, and Mrs. F. enjoyed it vastly, with one drawback, however. She was a New England woman, and accustomed to the domestic life of New England. Her house had always been a model of elegant nicety — her servants well trained and reliable, as a usual thing. To a person with her habits these slave-servants were almost intolerable. This, then, was the drawback — her *bête-noir* in the midst of so much that was delightful.

"The idea, Tom," she would say to her husband, "of being obliged to have six people to do what two could do at the North; and then of all the idle, careless, irresponsible creatures!"

The Colonel took it philosophically — laughed at their idleness, quoted the climate, their training or want of training, and told Mrs. F. that in Rome she must expect to do as the Romans did. Mrs. F. knew all this, and a good deal more about it than Tom did, and she knew it was a trial.

But one day she came in to dinner radiant. I believe she thought the worst of her troubles were over.

"Tom!" she said, in an exultant undertone as she stood by the window with him waiting for Major Luce to come in — "Tom, I've discharged Rose, and engaged a perfect jewel of a waiting-maid."

"You don't say so! Let's send out at once and have a cannon fired and the bells rung."

"Now, Tom, be serious and listen. She is a creole, and belonged formerly in a French family up the river, and does n't speak a word nor understand a word of English;" and Mrs. F. looked up in triumph as if the last item was the crowning virtue.

The Colonel laughed gayly. "That's the best of all, is it, Kate?"

"It is n't the least, Colonel Tom. Do you remember how Rose used to be found at key-holes sometimes?" answered Mrs. Tom, significantly.

Just here Major Luce came in, and the subject

was dropped as they turned to the dinner-table; but when they rose the Colonel, who could never spare his fun, took Luce aside and said lowly, but not so lowly but that Mrs Tom heard:—

"Luce, I want you to go down to the General and communicate a bit of news to him — it's a bell-ringing, cannon-firing affair, Luce, and I've no doubt he'll give orders"—

"Now, Colonel, you're too bad;" and Mrs. Tom, interposing, told the story herself; but the Colonel had his laugh, and that was all he wanted.

Four or five days passed, and nothing more was said about the new waiting-maid until one morning the Major asked, "How does Rose's successor get on, Mrs. F.?"

"Admirably. She's a perfect treasure, Major Luce. I knew I should like her in the beginning, she was so quiet and deft. Ah, Major, if you had ever had your muslins torn, and your laces lost, and your best silk dresses borrowed without your leave, you would appreciate what it is to be served by this Mathilde," concluded Mrs. F., with mock gravity.

The Major laughed.

"I dare say I should, Mrs. F.; but my muslins and laces are warranted not to tear or lose, and my best silk dresses don't fit anybody but myself."

Later on that same day they were all sitting in

the drawing-room, — Mrs. F. and the Colonel, and Miss Vescey — Mrs. F.'s sister, and Major Luce and two other officers who had dropped in for a call. It was getting late, and a wind had sprung up. Mrs. F. shivered with a little chill.

"Kate, you are taking cold; send for that paragon to bring your shawl," suggested the Colonel, in an aside.

When the paragon came in with the shawl he was busy talking again. Major Luce, who happened to be disengaged and looking that way, was probably the only person conscious of her personality as she entered. . "How well she carries herself!" he thought, vaguely. Then he glanced at her face. Below stiff folds of muslin, which concealed her hair, shone a pair of brilliant eyes, an olive cheek, and a mouth cut like Diana's, and curving beneath, a chin so firm, it was a trifle heavy.

"She looks like a picture; and where have I seen one like it?" mused the Major. "I know. In Valsi's studio at New York there's a Roman girl carrying a palm-branch, which she regards disdainfully. I used to think that Miss Laudersmine looked like it too, sometimes. Valerie Laudersmine. I wonder where she is now. *She* was a Louisianian — used to spend her winters at New Orleans. Handsome, haughty creature — how she would lift that proud head of hers if she knew I put her in comparison with a slave-girl! Heigh-ho! I suppose she's a rebel now. If she had been a man a pair of epaulets would have shone on her shoulders. And how soft she could be too, sometimes! I called her Valerie once — ah me!"

And in his recollection of Valerie Laudersmine he forgot Mathilde the waiting-maid.

The waiting-maid, however, as the days went on, continued to give unbounded satisfaction to her mistress. Nobody ever dressed hair like her; nobody was ever at once so deft and tasteful. Of course the Major forgot all about her; never thought of her again until again she recalled the picture in Valsi's studio, and so — Miss Laudersmine. He was playing backgammon with Miss Vescey in Mrs. F.'s little sitting-room up-stairs one morning, and glancing over · the board he could see Mathilde sitting sewing in the room beyond.

"Did you ever see that Roman girl in Valsi's studio, Miss Vescey?"

"Oh yes. It's a strange picture. I think."

"Did you ever notice that your new waiting-woman looks like it?"

"No, I never thought of it; but now you mention it, seems to me I do see the resemblance.

But you need n't speak so low, Major Luce ; she does n't understand a word of English."

" Oh, she does n't ! "

Presently Mrs. F. came in, and presently after coming in she wanted something which Mathilde must bring.

" Mathilde ! " and Mathilde came, quiet, soundless of foot, and prompt. She stood receiving the order, while the rest talked, oblivious of her. Major Luce was listening to Miss Vescey's description of the onyx ring she wore, and listening, was holding Miss Vescey's hand to look at the ring for the moment. He glanced up from the hand suddenly, and caught a pair of eyes that were not Miss Vescey's ; dark, brilliant, and piercing, they startled him with an odd sensation, like peril ; but as quickly as he met them they were withdrawn. As she left the room the influence seemed to pass, and he laughed at himself for it. He hardly thought of it again until the next day, as he was running up the stairs, he came upon her carrying a basket of flowers to her mistress's room. Two or three choice roses fell out at his feet, and he stooped involuntarily to pick them up. As he tossed them back he looked at her eyes again, but the lids were down, and her " *Je vous remercie* " was spoken in a swift nasal, and her whole air the very type of the class of slaves who are educated in the houses of the

French planters up the river. As she went in he met Mrs. F. coming out. He could say to Mrs. F. what he could n't to Miss Vescey, for besides being a great friend of his she was a married friend. Mrs. F. knew a good deal about his affairs, one way and another, and what he *had n't* told her she had guessed from what he *had* told. She knew about Valerie Laudersmine. She knew, that is, that, as the phrase goes, Miss Laudersmine and Major Luce had had a great flirtation, and that at the end of the summer, when she waited to hear of their engagement, that Luce suddenly disappeared, and only came back when Miss Laudersmine had left, and then with a gloomy face, and two or three bitter words that once or twice dropped from his lips. She had guessed the story, for she knew Valerie Laudersmine well enough to know how proud she was, and how high she looked ; and Everett Luce was not high enough for that looking. This was five years ago, and she supposed by this time that he had gotten over the whole affair, and perhaps forgotten Valerie Laudersmine.

In a moment she knew that he had n't forgotten her when he stopped her and said : —

" You remember Miss Laudersmine, Mrs. F. ? "

" Oh yes." And Mrs. F. looked curiously up at his face. It was cool enough.

" Have you ever thought," he went on, " that your waiting-maid resembles her in some ways ? "

" There ! " And Mrs. F. struck her two hands together in the sudden shock of thought. " There ! that is it ! I knew there was something — some resemblance to somebody."

They sat down together in the alcove of the bay-window in the hall, and by-and-by Luce said, with a wistful, grave simplicity that touched Mrs. F. greatly : —

" I never quite got over Valerie Laudersmine, Mrs. F. ? "

Mrs. F. said, in return, some kind, sympathetic, womanly things ; and under her spell he told her more of the affair than she had ever known before, and she found that she had not guessed wrongly.

" It is a long while ago — five years, Mrs. F. ; and I really thought the other day that I did n't care, you know, any more : but — just the turn of a girl's cheek and a pair of black eyes, and that old nerve I thought dead goes to vibrating again, and it aches confoundedly, Mrs. F., though I had the tooth drawn long ago."

He laughed, but it was a sad little laugh, sadder than any sigh to Mrs. F. Half ashamed of his confidence, he resumed : —

" I believe I am acting like a school-boy, or a fool, Mrs. F., but I am not going to say anything about it after this."

Mrs. F. assured him that he might say just as much as he pleased about it to her, and that he was neither a school-boy nor a fool in her estimation for what he had told her. But *she* had something to say now.

" There's one thing you have n't thought of, Major Luce — perhaps you never knew the fact. Valerie Laudersmine, when she was at Cape May that summer, had a waiting-maid who bore quite a curious resemblance to herself."

Major Luce's face was all aflame in an instant. He wheeled round.

" Who knows " —

" Exactly, Major Luce. Who knows but this girl is the quondam waiting-maid of Miss Laudersmine?   Shall I ask her now? "

" Yes, if you will, now and here."

Mrs. F. opened the door of her sitting-room and called " Mathilde ! "   Mathilde dropped the flowers which she was arranging and obeyed the call with her usual alacrity.   And as Major Luce looked again at this face which recalled another face the nerve he had fancied dead began to thrill again ; and it thrilled still more as he listened to the conversation that ensued.   It was in French, and the girl's voice was as he had heard it a while before — nasal and a trifle shrill, like her class, not like the dulcet tones of Valerie-Laudersmine, that soft-voiced siren who had sung his heart away five years ago.

"Mathilde," asked Mrs. F., "did you once belong to Miss Laudersmine?"

Mathilde looked open-eyed surprise as she answered, briskly, "*Oui, Madame.*"

"How long since?"

"Five years," after a minute's counting on her brown fingers, and with a stronger nasal than ever.

"And how came you to part from her?"

"Monsieur Laudersmine died, and Mademoiselle Valerie went to live with her uncle. It was an exchange, Madame. Madame Chesang wanted me, and offered Celie for me. Celie cannot dress hair like me; but Mademoiselle Valerie is good-natured, so she took Celie for me, Madame."

"Do you mean to say, Mathilde, that Madame Chesang, who used to live in this house, was your mistress before you came to me?"

"Yes, Madame."

"And that Monsieur Chesang is uncle to Miss Laudersmine?"

"Yes, Madame."

"Did you come straight from Monsieur Chesang's here? and was Miss Laudersmine there?" broke in Luce, in a slightly nervous tone.

"Oh no, Monsieur. Mrs. Chesang died three

years ago, and she gave me my freedom in her
will; then I came down to the city and hired out
as fine laundress. I have n't seen Mademoiselle
Laudersmine since, and I could n't tell where she
is, Monsieur," with a curious, stealthy look at Luce
from her piercing eyes.

There was no more to be learned from her after
this, and as soon as possible Mrs. F. dismissed her
back to her task. But after this Luce was no
more at rest. He could never see the slim,
straight figure, nor the olive curve of Mathilde's
cheek, nor the flash of her dark, brilliant eyes
beneath those folds of muslin, but it set his heart
to beating with old memories. One night she
passed him, unconscious of his presence, as he
stood in that very window-recess. The poise of
her head, the undulation of her movements was so
like, so very, very like!

" Confound the resemblance!" he said, under his
breath, and with an impatient stamp of his foot, a
bitter, troubled, vexed face. Then he turned and
looked after her. He saw her pass down the dim
corridor. He saw her half turn the handle of
a door, then pause, retrace her steps, and come
swiftly, softly back. It flashed over him in an unreasoning sort of way, just then, that Mrs. F. and
her sister were both away for the evening; at the
same moment he shrank involuntarily within the

embrasure. The next instant Mathilde flashed swiftly past his place of concealment and entered Mrs. F.'s room. And why not? He had seen her enter at that very door many and many a time. Why not now? There was no reason why not, to be sure; but a curious sensation oppressed him as he watched her; a sensation that was compounded of suspicion and peril; and he remembered the same sensation once before when he had first seen her.

One, two; the seconds ticked by, in audible throbs from the great hall clock, and still he waited, watching now for her reappearance, yet half jeering at himself for the indefinable fancies that held him there.

One, two; it seemēd an age. What was she about there so long? So long! Pshaw, it was but three minutes. Three minutes, in that time what might not be done?

"What a fool I am!" he muttered. "I believe I have been drinking too much champagne; I dare say the girl is putting her mistress's finery in order."

But hark! the door opens; there she comes, the gay coral ear-rings sparkling and tinkling; a smile lurking about her lips, which parting, hum swiftly a bit of the Marseillaise. How like the maid is to her quondam mistress! The old pang strikes the watcher in his nook as he sees her; and he sees, too, one shapely hand thrust into an apron pocket, and hears the rustle of paper, and is half ashamed of himself for the suspicion that upon so slight a footing gains ground. But as she passes out of sight he says, with a certain dogged resolution:—

"I 'll keep an eye on her any way; if there 's mischief I 'll find it out — but I wish she was n't so like, so very, very like."

And he did keep an eye on her. Twice that evening in the garden grounds he crossed her path with the careless pretext of smoking. Twice he cut off her egress from the private gateway. At the last she turned with a gesture, and half an exclamation that was impatience and disappointment all in one — the impatience and disappointment simply of a foiled coquette.

"Possibly no deeper errand than to meet her lover;" but as he made this inward remark he sighed satisfaction as he saw her flit up the stairway before him. By and by the Colonel and his wife and Miss Vescey came in. It was early yet, and a storm brooded in gusty sobs about the house; it brought damp and chill into the wide rooms, and Mrs. F., shivering under the influence, besought them to adjourn to her smaller boudoir, where Heckla should kindle a fire upon the hearth. Thither they went, and while Heckla, sable servitor, kindled a blaze which sent out aromatic odors of cypress and cedar, Miss Vescey brewed a beverage whose scents were of spices and wines. The scene so home-like and simple dispelled all fancies and suspicions, but still there was the possibility, and the Major told his story. The Colonel, shrewd soldier, was alert at once, listening intently and gravely; but Mrs. F., nettled at any distrust of her favorite, made jest of the whole affair. It was only some little French love-mottoes Mathilde was after, probably; she herself had told Mathilde where to find them; or it might have been a recipe for a cosmetic Madame Droyer had bestowed upon her, a most wonderful recipe for the hands; and Mathilde had a passion for concocting messes; and very likely, too, it was the young creole who kept the drug-shop round the corner whom Mathilde was seeking at the gateways.

Major Luce felt excessively annoyed at Mrs. F.'s annoyance; annoyed and a trifle disturbed at this jest-making.

Miss Vescey, cognizant of all this, tried to dispel it with the breath of a little song, airily chanted over her foamy distillation. A little French song, whose English

> " Heart, heart of mine,
> Why dost repine ? "

could scarcely give the impassioned aerial grace of

the original, which he had heard before. But it was the same lovely tune; and he could imagine as he bent his head away from the singer, and dipped his mustache into the warm sparkle of the spiced wine frothing up in his glass — he could imagine Valerie Laudersmine singing to him one summer night as they rowed down the river for lilies. Five years, and the lilies were all dead long ago — and Valerie, perhaps she too had followed the lilies. A sharp pang pierced him. Dead! he had not thought of that. Dead — all that life and bloom and beauty!

He looked up suddenly; it was a whisper through the song that caught his ear — just a " My shawl, Mathilde," and there she stood, for once unconscious, for once rapt, away and apart — betraying herself. There was wistful depth in her eyes, there was melting sweetness on her lips, as if she might then be singing softly the old French song : —

> " Heart, heart of mine,
> Why dost repine ? "

A little tinkling crash, a start and exclamations, while Mrs. F. moved her violet silk from the scene of accident, and then they all fell to laughing over the Major's preoccupation.

" Or was it Julia's song ? " bantered the Colonel.

" Yes, it was just that — Miss Julia's song," with a single glance at Miss Vescey, which cost

Everett Luce all his self-command; for over it flashed another glance, startled, yet, unafraid, which seemed to plead: "I trust you; *you* will not betray."

And while the others laughed and bantered he bent down to the fragments of his glass upon the floor, unheeding the reminder of Mrs. F. that Mathilde could perform that service; and bending there, his hands touched hers, and he knew that perhaps he held her life — Valerie Laudersmine's life — in his keeping. Valerie Laudersmine! All this time it had been Valerie Laudersmine, and he had not known. At first a thrill of delight, swift and unreasoning, at her simple presence; then fear, anxiety, foreboding, and suspicion, which deepened into horror, at the fate that might be — that must be — closing around them. He drew a deep breath at the thought that he *had* betrayed her; for, knowing now that it was Valerie Laudersmine, he knew no step of hers was purposeless in that house, nor that, left alone, she did other work than her own. What thwarted purpose was that in the garden then? What noiseless errand in the room beyond? And he had betrayed her! Betrayal — what did it mean? And this betrayal was assuredly of wrong and misdoing, of treason and conspiracy! What did his loyalty command him to do but to betray all treason and conspiracy?

His brain reeled with these questions, and his pulses throbbed dizzily, while still he bent there in such dangerous neighborhood, and still the laugh and bantering jest went on, and no one but they two conscious of the tragic undertone.

"Curious creature she is!" remarked the Colonel, as, the fragments gathered up, Mathilde moved stately from the room.

"A faithful creature!" interluded Mrs. F., with a little breath of malice. "See how she mends this old lace," holding up a web of Valenciennes.

"Lace? And how about that gold-lace on my coat, Mrs. F., which this 'faithful creature' was to rejuvenate with her wonderful fingers?" asked the Colonel.

"How about it? it's like new. You could never tell the broken thread; but look and see for yourself in the wardrobe in your room."

He came back with it on his arm, and, looking at it, fell into praises which satisfied even Mathilde's mistress.

"And the papers in the inner pocket I told you of, you put in my cabinet, I suppose, as I suggested?"

"No, not in the cabinet; it was that day I was ill in my room, and I dropped them in my writing-desk; or Mathilde did for me."

The eyes of Major Luce threw a startled, fearful

glance across the table; and there was something in the answering glance of his superior that fully met it. Just a moment of waiting, then the Colonel rose again. Mrs. F. looked up from the contemplation of her slippers on the fender.

"Wait, and I'll send Mathilde for the desk, Tom." But the Colonel had disappeared, and presently returning bore in his hands a little escritoire of gilt and inlaying.

"The key, Tom — underneath there. Don't you remember the small secret drawer outside for it?"

It was but a second that turning of the key, that lifting of the lid; but in the brief time what length of fear and dread, what fainting horror, possessed him who watched and waited from the other side of the little table, where still Miss Vescey brewed her posset and hummed her song. But the song was coming to an end, no more to be resumed that night. It broke off suddenly, in the turning of a note, at a new note in her brother-in-law's gay voice.

"Kate, Kate! what have you done?" It was not only displeasure, but it was the sharp, swift tone which bursts forth at only one crisis — that of peril or its anticipation. Then in an instant dismay seized upon the group there — in an instant they all knew what had happened, that Major Luce's suspicions had come true; but still in anx-

ious voice Mrs. F. cried, "What is it? what have
I done, Tom?"

"It was that plan of Gerritt's, Major, the whole
line of attack, and the present disposition of our
men in complete drawing;" but the Major, before
the Colonel had spoken more than the first half
dozen words, had disappeared.

He would save her yet from question or trial.
If he reclaimed the lost paper, what more for all
loyal purpose was needed? If he reclaimed it!

Down a wide hall, as he went out of Mrs. F.'s
boudoir, he caught the echo of a footstep. Following it, the flutter of a light garment led him on, and
on, still on, though a maze of doorways and passages until the fever of pursuit and delay nearly
maddened him. Then a voice — was it Mrs. F.'s?
— far off at first, then coming nearer, called "Mathilde, Mathilde!" — then other footsteps, other
voices, when suddenly a breath of the storm blew
coldly in from an opening door, and, following on,
he found himself in the garden grounds, out in the
wild tempestuous night. A late moon was struggling up through flying clouds, and by its fitful
light he discerned what he sought. There she fled
down the narrow, tortuous pathway which led to
the river-gate. A moment more and he held her
in his grasp — a moment more and he was speaking to her vehemently, almost incoherently, calling

her "Valerie;" imploring, beseeching, command-
ing in a breath. At the first words she knew the
danger; yet the reckless, adventurous spirit which
had incited her on to the part she had undertaken
still had possession of her. A strange exultant
look gleamed from her eyes.

"Well!" she exclaimed, in the breathless pause.

"The papers! give me the papers, Valerie! then
go free, and God help you!" he cried.

She seemed to start at the solemn passion of his
tone; but immediately her voice rang steadily in
answer : —

"At the foot of the garden, by the river-gate,
under the lion's head, there is a receptacle for letters — a cleft in the granite that will admit your
hand. I dropped the packet there an hour ago —
an hour hence it would have been beyond your
reach, if you had not prevented my egress from the
grounds; and so you checkmate me again, Sir."
She stepped forward, as if to go, but still his detaining hand lingered on her arm.

"Well, am I to go free, Sir?" in haughty accents.

What fate was it that held that moment? There
was no shadow of doubt of her in his mind as she
spoke; he believed she spoke only simplest truth,
and that in the cleft of granite he should find what
he sought; but some bitter pang of parting, some

anxious fear for her welfare in the wild and dreary night made him hesitate perhaps.

"But how can you go, where can you go alone, Val — Miss Laudersmine, at this hour?"

Again his tone seemed to touch her; and she lifted wistful eyes a moment and answered gentler than before : —

"I have friends who wait for me."

As she spoke, the wind rising in a fresh burst, a branch of the cypress under which he stood struck suddenly against her. Unprepared for the blow, she lost poise, reeled, and would have fallen but for her companion. As he caught her, something slipped from her hold and rustled to the ground. The moon came sailing up and showed him what it was — a slender packet sealed with red wax. Good Heaven! how well he knew it! And how bitter the recognition now; yet what Providence! As he stooped to take it their eyes met.

"Yes, I deceived you," she exclaimed bitterly, but with the bitterness of defeat solely. "I told you it was at the foot of the garden when I held it here in my hands. I meant to have gained time, as you see: an accident prevented me."

She stood as if waiting. She had deceived him. In how much more might she not even now be deceiving, misleading, and betraying? What was she to him? The woman whom he loved. But there was something else. There was his country and his honor ! Suddenly his mind cleared, and a divine resolution possessed him.

" Valerie — Miss Laudersmine, you are my prisoner."

The next instant lights gleamed from the opening doors, footsteps and voices rang — a confusion of question and exclamation and wonder. It seemed an age to Major Luce that he stood there with his hand closed over Valerie Laudersmine's slight wrist, until the soldierly figure of Colonel F. stood before them. At the first glance the Colonel saw the whole — the double identity, the deep-laid, thwarted purpose, and the pang of discovery. In another moment he saw, too, how much loyalty and honor meant with Everett Luce, as he noted the firm yet gentle hold of detention, and the stern sorrow of his face as he handed him the packet.

And Valerie Laudersmine was a prisoner in the house where she had fraudulently served. She uttered no complaint, she made no protest, she showed no sign of repentance, and none of anxiety through it all.

Quietly and even tenderly, for the sake of her youth and her sex, and perhaps, too, for the sake of the brave fellow who had so painfully proved his loyalty, the examination was carried on, and the final judgment awarded.   It was certainly gentle judgment, that sentence of banishment up the river, upon an unwilling *parole d'honneur.*   Gentle judgment for her sin; but she received it with the same cold, haughty apathy that had intrenched her from the first.

"I always thought her heartless — always," commented Mrs. F., with a pained, half-frightened face, after their last interview.

"And to think we should have been so deceived by a little disguising!" exclaimed Miss Vescey; "but there never was such an actress as Valerie Laudersmine.   The first time I ever saw her she played in Mrs. Althorpe's private theatricals, and how Charlie Althorpe raved about her!"

Heartless and an actress!   Perhaps they all judged her with this judgment except one, who might have been pardoned for even harsher judgment.   But he, as those dark eyes were lifted to his for the last time, realized what divine possibilities were lost in the warping realities of her education and associations, and what she might have been if all her life had not been spent under an unnatural rule, where every selfish whim was fostered, and every idle wish indulged.   Looking into her eyes, he said no word of reproach, but only with sad earnestness, —

"Good-by, Valerie."

She dropped her hand in his; it was icy cold, and her haughty voice faltered a little in replying:—

"You have done your duty, Major Luce, and I honor you for it."

In an instant, by that glance, by that faltering tone, he knew how near, yet how far apart they were; and he knew that when they parted it would be forever. But he had done his duty, and she honored him.

To Mrs. F. he said, one day:—

"I suppose I shall overlive this, and perhaps at some time be a happy and contented man, with altogether another future than this that I thought possible once; for neither men nor women give up their lives at one disappointment, however great, unless they are weak or wicked."   .

This was good and true philosophy; but it sounded a little too matter-of-fact and cool to Mrs. F., who remembered so vividly the sad passion of love which had broken up into every word and look a little while since from this now quiet speaker. She had not fathomed Everett Luce yet.

"He is n't a fellow to make a fuss about anything, but he is one to hold on to a feeling or a purpose a long time, Mrs. F.," commented that lady's husband.

And Mrs. F. realized how true this was as time went on and found Major Luce untouched by all the bright eyes and winning smiles that lavished their sweetness upon him.

THE RIBBON OF HONOR.

T HE night was very cold, and we had drawn up around the fire — an open fire of sea-coal, which the size of the room rendered necessary, even when the furnace was, according to Patrick, "at the top of its hate." We were a small party — my cousin, and my cousin's wife, her sister, Patty Emerson — a dark-eyed, Castilian-looking girl, whom you were constantly naming, in your imagination, Señora Inez, or Dolores; anything but the commonplace "Patty," to which she really responded — and Major Howith, an English friend of my cousin's and a charming person, easy, jovial, and sympathetic, and with a background of personal history which dated from the Crimea.

With myself we made just five, a group unequal as to whist, but quite equal to a much livelier pastime — story-telling. The Major, good fellow, had "opened the ball" with a "thrilling tale" or two from his Crimean experiences, and then for the first time we discovered that he was one of those heroes who had won the Victoria cross. Patty's eyes glistened.

"Oh, to think," she cried out, "that we here in America have gone through such a war, have had such splendid heroes, and not a national badge or a ribbon of honor to crown and specialize *our* special heroes!"

My cousin — who was himself something of a hero in the war, and whom we all called the Colonel, when we did not more affectionately and irreverently style him "Cousin Jim" — at this point gave utterance to an exclamation which at once aroused our interest.

"What is it, Colonel? — there 's a bee buzzing in your bonnet, that 's certain; and, as I 've told all my stories for to-night, you might as well open up your budget," put in Major Howith. We all joined in this invitation, or suggestion, and, after a minute or two, my cousin's pleasant voice was telling the story of the evening, — the story of " THE RIBBON OF HONOR."

"You remember Melroe?" he began, glancing at us three ladies. "He was the brightest, gayest little fellow, this Melroe," addressing himself to Major Howith, "the life of my regiment, and he had won his captaincy though he was but three-and-twenty. The night before his last battle, I recollect, was a specially merry evening all round, owing to Melroe's wit and humor and drollery. Dalzell, of the Fifteenth, and Melroe, had a tent together, and Hoyle and the two brothers Archy and Cam Browne, together with myself, were invited in that night to a little supper of Mel's giving. I recollect perfectly, as I went in, seeing Melroe bending over the oysters which he was cooking upon a spirit-lamp. He was great at all those things, and Cam Browne was running him as only Cam Browne could. 'You've missed your vocation, Mel; you should have been apprenticed to Soyer,' Cam was saying. 'You always had a knack at that kind of messing; and I remember,' turning to the rest of us, 'when he came a little urchin to school; and he actually, at that tender age, had furnished himself with sundry tin cups and various conveniences for brewing messes; and he was forever at it.' As I heard this I recalled the first time I met the youngster myself. I was at the same school, one of the seniors, and he was a little chap not yet turned into his teens, very fond of play, very fond of his tin-cup business, and very much afraid of ghosts. I used to meet him running down the corridors after dark. And once, I remember very well, when we were all in our rooms and the lights were being put out, how a little white face looked in, and a little, shaky voice cried, 'King, will you lend me your tooth-ache-drops?' I questioned the boy: 'Got the toothache, Mel?' 'No,' he answered, 'but Morty

has.' 'So you braved the ghosts for Morty's toothache,' I returned, viciously; 'and what's more,
to my thinking, the cold.' I told him I did n't
think I should crawl out of my warm bed on such
an errand, and that Jack Frost, the very whitest
ghost he ever saw, was waiting for him in that en-
try. The little chap flared up like a rocket. 'Do
you think I'd let a chap have a toothache for all
the ghosts in the world?' he cried out passion-
ately, winding up with, 'Oh, I hate you, big boys;
you're all so selfish!' I tried to mollify him by
offering to light him back, but he snatched the
drops and banged the door in my face; and I heard
him running down the dark corridor, gasping every
inch of the way for fear of the ghosts; and I know
of this little man's lying awake for hours one night
with his own toothache, which he bore rather than
brave the dark corridors! I told this story just
as I am telling it now to the fellows that night
in the tent, as we all stood and watched Melroe
at his oysters. I had a special reason for telling it. I knew very well that not a man in all
the regiment was so little understood as Holland
Melroe — perhaps so little appreciated. His estimate there that night, with those who liked him
heartily, too, was of a gay, good-humored fellow,
who took his soldier's life as easily as was consistent with a good deal of laziness, and a little shrink-

ing from any active service. I felt sure that I read
him better than this, and that beneath this exterior
of laziness and shrinking there lay noble qualities
of courage and valor. As I finished my story that
night, Dalzell called out, 'You ought to have had
a medal for overcoming your dragon, Mel.' 'Or
a *cordon bleu*,' Cam Browne suggested. From
that they all fell to talking of the foreign system of
badges and medals of honor, and one of the young
men pulled out of his pocket, I recollect, a 'Corn-
hill Magazine,' and read to us Thackeray's Rounda-
bout paper 'On Ribbons.' The final summing up
of the talk was in great agreement with Thackeray,
and the general conclusion that we ought to have
a 'ribbon of honor,' 'not simply a Kearny cross,
but a grand *cordon bleu*, or a medal coming straight
from the heart and hand of that grand old fellow,
Abraham Lincoln,' Dalzell burst out. 'Of course
we 're all too modest to ever expect to be decked in
that way, but how many of us would disdain it?'
he concluded.   •

"As the talk deepened, Melroe's face had lost
its gayety, I noticed. He drew a deep sigh as Dalzell spoke, and a wistful look came into his eyes.
I could guess pretty well how it was with him.
What was *he*, beside them? What brilliant, or
courageous, or soldierly, or spirited qualities had
he? These men would easily win their *cordon*

bleu, for they were *without fear.* Without fear! That was what was in his mind, as he very shortly confessed, by a blundering, honest question bearing directly upon the subject. How did it feel to be without fear? Every man of them knew of this little white ghost of Melroe's, yet every one of them knew that he never had failed to do his duty. They had laughed quietly together over it, and said: 'Mel is a good fellow; he never will run away, but he will never distinguish himself — that is certain.' And now suddenly with his question arose another with them: How came he here into this voluntary service with this characteristic? But before asking it they answered his query, one and another smiling, yet serious and truthful.

"At their first battle? yes, it had been a shock, and then it was over. Various emotions assailed them now. but none of fear. But how was it with him? they asked. They all knew something how it was, as I have said, but not wholly, until he burst out impulsively : —

"'Well, to tell the truth, boys, I will own that I am awfully afraid every time, to this day, and I can't get over it.'

"'But how came you here, anyway, with that feeling, and being here why do you stay?' asked Cam Browne.

"For a moment there was a look of surprise on

Melroe's face, — a look as if he doubted whether he had heard aright.

"'How came I?' he uttered, slowly; 'how could I stay at home? A man can't choose at such a time. If I saw an assassin enter my friend's house, while he lay sleeping, I might be very much afraid of the assassin, but I could n't very well go on my way in safety, and tell some other man to go forward to the rescue. I might recoil from the encounter, but I should recoil ten times more from the skulking away from it. No,' he went on, 'I thought this all over; I knew it would hurt, — this kind of life, — but I concluded it would hurt a great deal more to turn my back upon it. Why, believing as I do, you know, a fellow could n't.' I can see Hoyle, and Dalzell, and the two Brownes, exchange glances here. They two, ay, and every one of them there, I knew, thought of the story of the boy at school, even then manfully fighting his ghosts for his principle. Those of us who had smiled at this ghost, and said, 'Mel is a good fellow; he never will run away but he never will distinguish himself — that is certain,' now, in contemplation of this courageous cowardice, felt inclined to doff our hats to the simple, manly fellow we had underrated, and to ask his pardon. But there was little said in acknowledgment or praise; it was a tender subject, involving this foregone lighter estimate; but there were warmth and friendliness in the 'good-nights,' which conveyed to him a sense of sympathy, an assurance to his modest mind that he had not spoken too freely. I remember Cam Browne said laughingly as he left the tent, 'After all, Captain, you may win your *cordon bleu* before any of us yet.'

"They were light words spoken hastily, out of the warm, kind heart of the young officer, as a good-natured remark to evince his belief in that moral courage that he admired.. Light words, and even while they were being spoken, perhaps fate was weaving that destiny which should make them no longer light words in the memory of us who listened to them.

"The next day we fought the battle of Chancellorsville. Toward the latter part of the day, when defeat was beginning to stare us in the face, after the earlier promise of victory, which combined and splendid action and the most untiring gallantry had given, I received a message from Major Dalzell to send a reënforcement to the left wing, where Captain Melroe and himself were endeavoring to hold their ground and save their colors. I had only a handful of men that I could ill spare, but I sent them immediately, for I knew that Dalzell would not have applied for help unless he had great need. Immediate action being suspended for a time on my right, I had a brief opportunity to observe the movements of the left. As I looked through my glass, I saw Dalzell advance with his column, not a large body of men, but compact and in order. A heavy roar of musketry met them; still they kept on, though I could see that the raking fire had told. The next charge was more fatal. As the smoke cleared, the lamentable effect was obvious. More than one gallant fellow had fallen; among them their leader, Dalzell. The column began to waver. The consequence at this particular point of a panic and a rout would be especially disastrous. I rose in my saddle with my excitement. 'Ah,' I thought, 'if I could only dash forward to the rescue!'

"At that moment I saw that a new leader had arisen. I saw him rush forward, I saw him glance back to the broken, wavering ranks, I saw him beckon them on with his sword, and, more than all, by an attitude of command that impressed me even then. At sight of him the wavering ranks closed in, and dashed forward, with a shout that reached me where I watched, and which I knew meant victory or death. A few moments later the Sixteenth came up to reënforce the right wing, and I had the liberty to ride forward. Melroe, — for you have guessed that he was the leader who took Dalzell's place, — Melroe, by his magnetic leadership, his dash and spirit, had saved his colors, and won, for his men at least, a famous victory, one of those side-issues of success which go far to ameliorate the greater defeat.

"But it was a victory I did n't feel much like rejoicing in, as I saw Melroe himself lying on a little hillock, shot through the heart. The color-sergeant — a little Irish fellow — had dragged him to the upland where he lay, and as I approached, he took off his cap, more in honor to the dead than to me and said chokingly : —

"'See that, Colonel; he seized 'em out of my hand as I was tuk, dizzy-like, with this scratch on my forehead, and when I came to myself, he had got his death a-saving of me and the flag, sir.'

"The little sergeant had laid the colors upon the dead breast of his officer as tenderly as a mother might strew flowers upon her child. Cam Browne just then joining me, I pointed to the sad spectacle. Cam bent over and touched the tattered remnants that meant so much, and had cost so much. 'He has won his *cordon bleu!*' he said, significantly. Yes, he had won his *cordon bleu*, the brave little fellow, fighting a double enemy every inch of the way." The Colonel paused a moment, and took out an old memorandum-book ; opening it, he drew forth something that seemed of many colors, a strip either of paper or silk, only a few inches in length and breadth. "This," he resumed, "is a piece of that *cordon bleu.* It was wet with his blood when I took it, and I have kept it ever since, for I knew no one else who was nearer to Melroe than myself, for he was an orphan, and without brothers or sisters. If he had had a sweetheart, I would have sent it to her, that she might have known what a hero she had lost in this young fellow, whose delicate, sensitive nature shrank from the conflicts which his great soul urged him into. I have seen many brave charges, many forlorn hopes carried, since that day, Howith, but I never saw a braver charge or a more forlorn hope carried than this that led Melroe to his death. We mourned Dalzell, good fellow, but there was something in the loss of Melroe that went beyond every other loss. We loved him better than we knew, and when we buried him there every one of us recalled that sentence of his, 'I might recoil from the encounter, but I should recoil ten times more from the skulking away from it.'"

A momentary silence fell upon us all as the Colonel ceased. But as he closed his memorandum-book, shutting in the strip of blood-stained, faded silk, a voice broke the silence : —

"James, give it to me — Holland Melroe's *cordon bleu!*" ·

"You, Patty?"

" Yes, to me, James," Patty answered, quite steadily, though white as the dead.

Mechanically, perhaps instinctively, the Colonel held out the sacred memento without a word. But the Colonel's wife had no such delicate instinct of the truth.

" What do you mean, Patty ? " she exclaimed.

" I mean," returned Patty, with great dignity, " that I have a better right to Holland Melroe's *cordon bleu* than any one else ! "

" O Patty ! and all the time you were " — But Mrs. King's discretion at this point came back to her ; it was too late, however, to serve her purpose.

" Yes, Emily ; all the time I was engaged to Morton Eames ! But you know who brought me into that. It was scarcely my own doing, and Holland Melroe never sought me after he discovered that my word was passed to another. But, before he discovered this, I knew his heart and mine. When I got news of his death I broke my engagement to Morton, but I could not go talking about Holland then. I had no right to tell the truth then who could not tell it before, — who had to be told by death what the whole truth meant even to myself."

By this time we had all been brought up, as it were, to Patty's revelation — all but Mrs. King. I noticed vaguely that she looked disturbed, and glanced uneasily at Major Howith. But for that I should have forgotten his presence, yet even then he did not seem an intruder, stranger though he was. The Colonel, always fond of his little sister Patty, as he called her, found new cause for tenderness now. She had been Melroe's sweetheart — Melroe, whom he had loved? And, leaning forward, he took her in his arms and kissed her.

The next morning I got the meaning of Mrs. King's disturbance. She came into my room, with the words : —

"Just think of Patty's making such a mess of it ! "

"What do you mean?" I inquired, thoroughly amazed.

"Oh dear! what do I mean? Don't you see that Major Howith was immensely pleased with Patty? And now, just for that old sentimental nonsense being dragged up, it will fall through, for he is not the man to play second fiddle to any other man, dead or alive. And it would have been such a match for Patty!" wound up the fascinating but worldly Mrs. King.

I turned upon her all the vials of my wrath. Patty had come out most nobly, and she ought to be ashamed if she could n't appreciate such nobility,

I declared. But I did no good; she only reiterated her regrets at Patty's "mess," not a whit disturbed by my vials of wrath. In this iteration she was cut short by her husband's voice, as he came in from the little library which communicated with the room we occupied.

"Emily, you don't know men quite as well as you think you do, my dear. When I went into the smoking-room last night Major Howith joined me; and what do you think he said to me?"

"Well, what?" inquired Mrs. Emily, making a little impatient movement.

"He said that if Patty was to be won by any living man he should try his best to win her. You see, my dear, your way of looking upon things does n't always fit the case and the people. Howith is a man to appreciate just such silent endurance and faithfulness as Patty revealed, and he does n't believe that her heart is forever buried in Melroe's grave any more than I do. It was my story of Mel that made everything fresh and living to her again. And now, Mrs. Emily, don't you talk this over to Patty — not a word, mind, or you may never have Major Howith for a brother-in-law!"

Mrs. Emily laughed.

"Oh, I can keep a secret when I like as well as Patty, and I 'll keep this; and I 'm glad your sentiment has turned out better than my sense this time, Sir!" she retorted, gayly.

Her husband laughed, too; but he looked at her, I thought, a little sadly, as he replied : —

"Ah, Em! perhaps you will see some time that our sentiment, as you call it, is better than your sense."

But she never will!

.   .   .   .

It was four years after this conversation — four years almost to a day that I went down to the St. Denis one bright morning to call upon Mrs. Felix Lundy Howith, who has just arrived from England on a three months' visit. Before I left her, a sweet-faced English girl came bringing in a sweet-faced half-English and half-American baby of two years, though he looked for all the world as much like a young Castilian as his dark-eyed mother.

"And what is his name?" I asked.

"Holland — Holland Melroe Howith. Felix named him, and he would have it so. Was n't it superb of him? But Felix *is* superb — you never saw such a man, dear, as Felix!"

I told my cousin, the Colonel, of this conversation. He looked at his wife, that pretty, light-natured, fascinating little Emily.

"Here 's our sentiment against your sense, Mrs. Emily. You see how well it works."

"Yes, I see," she answered ; "but" — laughing in our faces — "I was right in one thing: I told you the Major was n't the man to play second fiddle, and he is n't. He assigns that part to his son, you see!"

www.ingramcontent.com/pod-product-compliance
Lightning Source LLC
Chambersburg PA
CBHW020945120726

47905CB00008B/2685